The Boy Who Was Kissed

by

T. J. Baer

Cover Art by *Lisa Dawn MacDonald*

The Wild Rose Press, Inc.
PO Box 708
Adams Basin, NY 14410-0708
Visit us at www.thewildrosepress.com

Publishing History
First Edition, 2024
Trade Paperback ISBN 978-1-5092-5485-9
Digital ISBN 978-1-5092-5486-6

Published in the United States of America

Dedication

For all the queer kids. This one's for you.

Chapter One

"Dad, calm down, I'm not gonna be late."

Dad wipes his hands on his sunny yellow apron and sets a plate of pancakes on the table in front of me. As he takes off the apron, his "Proud Black Nerd" T-shirt earns a few more stains from his flour-speckled fingers.

"I'm perfectly calm," Dad says in his usual measured tones. "I just think you might want to consider the fact that you're still in your pajamas, sitting down for breakfast, when you have to be at school in—"

"Twenty-five minutes. I know. It's plenty of time, I promise." I shove a too-large bite of fluffy, syrupy goodness into my mouth and chew. "Anyway, I'm the new guy. If I show up late, I can always say I got lost or something."

Dad rolls his eyes, but he's smiling. It's good to see, honestly. There were months after Mom left when he practically never smiled, but now it's like he's finally getting back to who he was before. Or maybe this is a new him, a better him. I hope this year I can be a better me, too.

"Fine." He lifts his hands in classic *well, I tried* fashion. "You're almost seventeen, and you're clearly far too old to need your dear old dad's advice. Just don't come crying to me if you end up in detention on your first day."

"In the unlikely event I get detention, I promise to

keep my tears far away from you."

"Much appreciated," Dad says dryly.

Despite my words, I wolf down my breakfast in three minutes flat, deposit the empty plate in the dishwasher, and thunder up the stairs to my room to get dressed. I'm pretty nervous, to be honest, and not just because this is my first day at a new school in a completely new town.

Because I'm finally going to see him. I've been dreading and dreaming of this moment for years, and it's actually here. It almost doesn't feel real.

I want to just throw on any outfit like I don't care how I look, but who am I kidding? I debate a few options and settle on an orange T-shirt, gray zip-up sweatshirt, and jeans miraculously free of holes. I give my black curls a quick finger-comb, cram books, notebooks, and a worn cloth pencil case into my backpack, and then there's nothing to do but go.

Dad finds me standing by the front door a few minutes later, my backpack hanging from my shoulder and my jaw tight as I try to convince my fingers to turn the knob. His hand settles on my shoulder and gives it a gentle squeeze.

"I can give you a ride, if you want."

Some of the nerves melt away, and I throw him a lopsided smile over my shoulder. "It's okay, Dad. I got it."

He opens the door for me, and I head out into the driveway to the old clunker car Uncle Ronnie gave me for my birthday last year. It's an absolute piece of crap, but I don't think I've ever loved anything more.

"Drive safe, Jasper!" Dad shouts from the porch. I toss him a wave as I climb into the clunker and coax the engine into starting up.

Gravel crunches under the wheels of the car, and I'm off, rattling down the back roads of Nelson Springs, Illinois, toward the boy whose life I ruined six years ago.

****

My pulse thrums in my ears as I pull into a parking space in the student lot.

I've envisioned this moment so many times, but now that I'm actually here, all my doubts and fears surge to the surface. *He's never going to forgive me. What if he doesn't even want to talk to me? Six years is a long time. What if he punches me? What if he has a boyfriend? What if his boyfriend punches me?*

I force myself to breathe slowly and evenly, counting my breaths, talking myself down from my panic like I used to talk Felix down from his.

It works.

I take one final fortifying breath, grab my backpack from the passenger seat, and head for the front doors of Nelson Springs High.

I'm not late, but I'm not early either, and there are a lot of kids milling around the halls, retrieving books from their lockers, talking to their friends, or leaning sleepily against the wall staring at their phones. My eyes snap to the face of every person I pass, but none of them are Felix.

I pass a bulletin board full of notices, one of which is a rainbow-colored poster about a lunchtime Queer Straight Alliance meeting today in room 215. My locker reveals itself a few steps later, and it takes me three tries to open it because I keep glancing over my shoulder and messing up the combination.

I've just finished dumping in my afternoon books

when a blur of movement catches my eye, and I turn to see a locker five or six down from mine swinging open. When it swings shut, I stare straight into Felix Morales's brown eyes.

There's a moment of blankness on his face, and then his eyes widen, and his mouth opens, and I know he's about to say my name. I *know* it. I can't get over how tall he is now, taller than me, or how I glimpse tan biceps beneath the sleeves of his T-shirt, muscled legs beneath his loose, sporty blue shorts. His face has lost its childhood roundness and is all chiseled angles, and his hair is longer, hanging in soft waves around his face. Felix in fifth grade was scrawny and awkward, all shy smiles and polite stammering, but the Felix in front of me now is as far removed from that as I can imagine.

But his eyes are the same, soft and brown and staring into mine like he can see into the deepest heart of me. Fear and joy war in my chest, and I wait for him to say my name, to ask what I'm doing here—

But he turns and walks away.

Numb with shock, I watch as he trades greetings and fist bumps with a bunch of athletic looking guys, and a girl with a long, honey-blond ponytail slides her arm around him and leans her head against his shoulder as they walk. I don't jolt out of my daze until the first bell rings, and then I gather up my books and my wounded heart and trudge to first period.

Chapter Two

As I slide into a desk near the back of the classroom, my fingers stray to my lips like I can still feel the phantom brush of Felix's against them. When I realize what I'm doing, I force my hand down to my side.

Okay, this is fine. I hurt Felix, hurt him very badly, and it makes sense he wouldn't want to talk to me. A part of me hoped he would wave away my apologies and we could go back to some version of what we were before, but the rest of me was pretty sure it wouldn't be that easy—that he'd need to be convinced I'm a good guy now.

But to totally ignore me? To look at me, *into* me, and then walk away like none of it matters? It's hard to take. It makes me wonder, for the first time since I hatched this plan, if maybe I don't deserve his forgiveness. If maybe it's better if I just leave him alone and forget about trying to make amends for the horrible thing I did to him in fifth grade.

I scan every face in my English class, but none of them belong to Felix. The teacher manages to butcher my name, calling me "Jason St. Clair," and I correct her with a polite, "It's Jasper Sinclair," while snickers echo through the room.

After the attendance is finished, the teacher asks us to split into twos for some kind of icebreaker exercise. I end up paired with the guy sitting next to me, a huge football player type with short black hair who looks like he could snap me in half without breaking a sweat.

I throw him a nervous glance. "Uh, hey."

I'm expecting a gruff, one-word answer or maybe a roll of the eyes, but he full-on beams at me. "Hey, new kid!"

His voice is bright and cheerful, his big hand swallowing up my smaller one and shaking it enthusiastically up and down.

I choke out a nervous laugh as he releases my fingers. "I'm Jasper."

"Not Jason." His eyes are warm and dark and sparkling with amusement, and his shirt, which I thought was just a plain green polo, turns out to have a tiny, embroidered frog on the left pocket. "Honestly, don't worry about Ms. Keeley. She called me Carmen for a good three weeks last year. It's Cameron, by the way. Cam for short."

"Not Carmen. Got it."

I watch him write his name across the top of his paper—*Cameron Matsumoto-Rogers*.

"Mouthful, right?" he says. "I wanted to just go by Cameron Rogers for a while, but apparently that's betraying my 'proud Asian heritage,' so my mom put a stop to it pretty quick. But try being a five-year-old in kindergarten and having to learn to spell all that."

I write my name on my own paper, but I've barely finished when Cameron snatches the paper off my desk and scribbles something. When he hands it back to me, I see he's written "Not Jason" below my name in neat block letters.

"Just so Ms. Keeley doesn't forget," he says with a wink.

We start on the exercise, which involves asking each other all kinds of random invasive questions.

"So uh, question one." I squint at the paper until the words come into focus. "What was a defining moment of your childhood?"

Cameron furrows his thick, dark eyebrows and taps his chin. "Defining moment. Defining moment..." He slaps his hand palm-down on the table. "Chicken nuggets."

There's a long silence.

I shift closer, like proximity might make the words make sense. "Chicken nuggets?"

"Yep."

I dutifully write "chicken nuggets" on my paper, then lay down my pencil and fold my hands on the desk. "And do you want to expand on that, or..."

He leans forward in his chair. "Right, so I'm about nine years old. I'm on a road trip with my family, and my little sister and I are being absolute brats. Pulling each other's hair, kicking the back of my mom's seat, whining about anything and everything. And then my mom sees the Golden Arches and pulls us into the drive-through, and suddenly we're all excited because we freaking live for the nugs. We can *taste* them. My mom pulls up to the window and orders nuggets and a shake, and my sister and me are there wondering why she only ordered one when there's three of us.

"And my mom, get this, she pulls us into a parking spot, and while my sister and I are there in the backseat staring at her—she eats every single nugget, drinks the shake, and then pulls out and starts driving again."

I burst out laughing. "Man, that is savage."

"Right? My little sis and I were in tears, and Mom

didn't say a word, just wiped the crumbs off her mouth and kept driving. And I mean, she did feed us—she'd packed a bunch of sandwiches and stuff for us to eat—but you try enjoying a ham and cheese sandwich when you can still smell those sweet, sweet nugs in the air."

"Sounds like torture."

"Oh, it was. Anyway, that's my defining moment because it taught me two things. First, it taught me not to be a little punk when I didn't have to be, and second, it taught me my mom is a freaking badass and I should never mess with her, ever."

I laugh again and write as neat a summary of that as I can.

Cameron hefts his own paper. "Right, your turn. Defining moment. Wow me."

"Not sure I can compete with chicken nuggets."

"Well, of course not, but do your best."

I open my mouth but close it again just as quickly, my gaze dropping to the scratched wood of the desk. I know what my defining moment is, but the idea of putting it into words—of telling Cameron, even vaguely, about the worst thing I've ever done in my life—makes me want to crawl under my desk and hide until the bell rings.

"Hey." Cameron's voice is soft, and when I turn, his face is inches from mine. "You okay?"

Real concern shines from his eyes, and I'm momentarily stunned that someone I've just met actually cares this much. I manage a strained smile. "Yeah, just… There's definitely a moment that comes to mind, but I don't think it's something I want to tell Ms. Keeley about."

"Well, you can always pick a different one. Or make

one up. You're the mysterious new kid—maybe your defining moment was when your CIA agent father taught you how to fire a gun at age eight or something."

I snort. "My dad's a tech nerd who judges cosplay competitions on the weekends."

Cameron raises a finger. "Or is that just what he wants you to think?"

Somehow, I'm laughing again, momentary angst forgotten. I've spent five minutes with this guy, and I've laughed more than I have in the last six months.

We make our way through more of the questions, skipping my defining childhood moment for now since I need more time to come up with a school-appropriate answer. I learn that Cameron actually has two younger siblings—the sister, now fourteen, who was present for the nugget incident, and a little brother who's just turned three. His mom, aside from being a nug-eating badass, is a single parent who runs a little café and apparently makes the best pastries in the world.

"So it's not that I'm doubting you," I say.

"Good, because you shouldn't."

"Right. But if you haven't tried all the other pastries in the world…"

"Then how can I know hers are the best?" Cameron steeples his fingers and leans back in his chair. "Trust me. You try hers, and you just know. I can bring some in tomorrow, but only if you think you can handle it."

"Handle what?"

"The knowledge that no other food will ever live up to what you're about to taste, and you'll spend the rest of your life being disappointed by everything else you eat."

He holds the deadly serious expression for a few more seconds, then grins and ducks his head.

"Nah, I'm just messing with you. My mom's pastries really are good, though."

Pastries lead us to talking about our favorite breakfasts, and we're just wrapping up a laughing argument on whether sweet or savory is better when the bell rings, cutting me off midsentence in my defense of team savory. I blink like I've been jarred out of a dream and glance at my half-empty paper.

"Er, I guess we got a little sidetracked."

Cameron shrugs as he gets to his feet. "It's not due 'til tomorrow. We can always finish it up later." He lifts his eyebrows. "Or make stuff up. You sure you don't want your dad to be a secret agent?"

"Pretty sure I wouldn't be allowed to write it in a school report if he was."

"Fair enough. What have you got next?"

I dig my schedule out of my pocket and squint at it. "Ugh, math."

"Not a fan?"

"I hate it. I suck at math."

To my surprise, he slings his arm around my shoulder and gives me an encouraging squeeze, and it only feels a little like I'm being crushed by a friendly bear. "If I tell you I suck at it worse, will that make you feel better?"

"Maybe?"

He winks at me. "Well, bad news then because I'm awesome at math. But at least we're in the same class. I won't let you copy my answers, but maybe I can help you if you get stuck."

As we make our way down the hall, Cameron says hi to almost everyone we pass, and almost everyone we pass has a friendly word or a wave for him, too. I peer at him from the corner of my eye and wonder who the hell this giant, illogically friendly guy is, but mostly I'm just grateful for whatever's possessed him to adopt me. Maybe it won't last, maybe he's just being polite to the new kid, but for now, I feel more relaxed and comfortable than I ever did at my old school.

Cameron and I turn out to have almost identical schedules, so when lunchtime rolls around, I'm trying to figure out how to sneak off to the Queer Straight Alliance when he says,

"I'm heading to the QSA meeting for lunch, but I can catch up with you in Biology."

I nearly trip over my own feet. "You're in the QSA?"

"You sound surprised."

"I guess I figured you'd be, like, on the football team or something…"

He barks out a laugh. "Yeah, no. Football is definitely not for me. But even if it was, who says a person can't be on the football team and in the QSA?" There's a playful sparkle in his eyes, and I admit he has a point. "Anyway, the QSA's a great group, and we always have a ton of fun there. Plus, the school buys us pizza for the first meeting of the year, so I might have some tiny ulterior motives there, too." He casts me a careful glance. "You can come too if you want, though I know it's not for everybody. But you really don't have to be queer to go. Lots of straight people are members, too."

"I'm not straight," I blurt out, and Cameron blinks at me in surprise. So do the four or five people walking ahead of us in the hallway. My cheeks warm as I avoid their stares. "I mean, I was actually planning to go to the meeting anyway, so maybe I can go with you?"

Cameron gifts me another thousand-watt grin, and instead of wrapping his arm around my shoulders, he grabs my hand and drags me down the hallway after him, bellowing for people to get out of the way as we go.

As we stagger into room 215, laughing and out of breath, a rush of nerves shoots through me. Somehow Felix wasn't in a single one of my morning classes, but he's sure to be here for the QSA meeting.

"This your first time at a meeting like this?" Cameron asks in an undertone. His expression is all friendly compassion, his voice gentle.

I tuck my sweaty palms into my pants pockets and try to pretend my heart isn't hammering against my ribcage. "Um, yeah actually. I wasn't really out at my old school."

"Well, you don't have to be out here, either, if you don't want. Like I said, there are plenty of straight people here, too."

I want to ask where he falls on the sexuality spectrum, if he's here as an ally or a fellow member of the queer community, but it doesn't seem right to ask. And with how open Cameron is about everything, I can't imagine it'll stay a secret for too much longer.

Room 215 is just a regular classroom with a chalkboard, teacher's desk, and the standard rows of student desks, though as Cameron and I enter, a handful of people are dragging the desks into a large semi-circle. Cameron doesn't hesitate before joining them, grabbing one desk in each big arm and sliding them effortlessly into the desired positions.

A pretty Black girl with thick dark hair down to her shoulders laughs and squeezes his bicep, and I walk up to them just in time to hear Cameron say, "—here for the pizza."

The girl rolls her eyes. "Yeah, I'm sure that's your only reason for being here. I'm sure being our freaking president doesn't have anything to do with it."

I gape at him. "You're the president? Of the QSA?"

Cameron tosses a sly smile over one shoulder. "Did I forget to mention that?"

The girl spares me a glance as she finishes writing "Queer Straight Alliance" on the board in rainbow-colored chalk. "Unanimously elected at the end of last year, first junior ever to hold the position." She wipes her chalk-dusty hand and holds it out to me, and I take it. Her fingers are warm and lotion-soft. "I'm Raven, by the way."

My eyebrows lift. "Raven? That's such a cool name."

"Thanks, I picked it myself." At my confusion, she points to a little badge on her chest that has a picture of the trans flag and bold black letters that say, "she/her." "So do you have a name, or should I just make one up?"

"It's not Jason," Cameron says.

"Jasper," I say. "I'm new. I just moved here, I mean. Me and my dad."

Raven is about my height, five eight or five nine, and she looks soft and pretty in a white blouse and black pleated skirt but is also wearing the most kick-ass pair of purple combat boots I've ever seen. "Well, I hope you'll feel at home here," she says. "There's no pressure to say anything about your identity if you don't want to, but just know that you can, anytime. Same with pronouns. We have some name tags over on the desk, and you can write your name and pronouns on them if you want to, but no pressure. It's all about feeling comfortable here."

"Are you sure you're not the president?" I ask her.

Raven lifts a finger. "Vice president. Which means I do all the real work."

"I'm just the figurehead, really," Cameron says. "And for the record, I fully agree Raven would make a way better president than me, but she insisted on running for vice president instead."

She shudders. "Please, I have no desire for the spotlight. And this way, you get to deal with all the public speaking and social stuff you're so good at, and I get to work in the shadows quietly getting stuff done while everyone is focused on you. Perfect partnership."

A pair of girls come in with the pizzas soon after that, followed by a lanky blond kid with a "Lars, they/them" sticker on their chest and two family-sized bottles of soda cradled in their skinny arms. The smell of the pizza starts a hunger-related eruption in my stomach, and it seems like a very long time since my hurried breakfast with Dad.

There are quite a few other people now, a lot of them standing around talking to each other, some sitting quietly at the desks like I am. Cameron heads to the front of the room, and it only takes him clearing his throat once for the group to fall silent.

"So hey, everybody, welcome to another year at the QSA!"

A cheer goes around the room. I smile and join the clapping.

"I won't say too much since I know you're all really here for the pizza, but I hope this'll be another great year for us. After this week, we'll be meeting every Friday like usual and planning all kinds of fun events, so make sure you pick up a copy of the calendar while you're stuffing your faces. Okay, that's all from me. Get that pizza!"

Another cheer, this one peppered with laughter, and the group meanders to the front of the room and the pizza boxes waiting there. I hang back, glancing around at the crowd.

"Looking for somebody?" It's Cameron, looking flushed after his bout of public speaking but as upbeat as ever.

"Uh, yeah actually. Felix Morales? I don't know if you know him, but—"

Cameron's smile slips, and my stomach drops with it. "Felix? Nah, he wouldn't be caught dead at a QSA meeting."

"Really? Why not?"

Cameron studies my face. "Are you friends with him?"

"No," I say, which is the truth. "I knew him back when we were kids, that's all, and I thought he might be here."

"Well, sorry to be the one to tell you this, but Felix is a massive homophobe."

The words knock the breath out of my lungs. "What? But...he can't be."

Cameron grimaces. "Afraid there's a lot of evidence to the contrary. He's pretty loose with the gay jokes, especially in the locker room, and he and his buddies egged the QSA booth at the spring festival last year. He might be an awesome soccer player, but the guy is really not an ally."

I slump into the nearest chair. "But...he kissed me."

The words just fall out. I'm not even aware I've said

them out loud until Cameron is kneeling in front of me with wide eyes.

"He *what*?"

I open my mouth, close it again, then glance at all the people milling around us. Cameron follows my gaze and gives a curt nod.

"It's none of my business, so I won't ask follow-up questions even though I really, really want to. But if you do want to talk to somebody about it…"

I do, I realize. I really do.

I stare into his warm, dark eyes and manage a weak smile. "Any chance you're free after school today?"

A slow grin forms on his face. "I'm supposed to help my mom out at the café, but if you want to come along, I'll treat you to a pastry or something?"

"Well, I'm not going to turn down a free pastry."

He claps me on the shoulder, and we head to the front to get our pizza before everyone else devours it. I eat, I talk to Cameron and Raven, I meet new people, I write, "Jasper, he/him" on a name tag and stick it to my chest. But all the time, I keep thinking, *Felix, what the hell happened to you?*

Chapter Three

It's called Mama's Little Café, and it might be the cutest place I've ever seen in my life. The tables are white, the chairs hot pink. Fairy lights drape across the walls, and cheerful Japanese pop pumps out of the speakers. The pastry case is stuffed full of brightly colored cupcakes and sweet buns that look like adorable animals—pandas, cats, dogs, foxes—and painted across the back wall is a chibi anime-style drawing of a woman in an apron with her hair in a bun and a welcoming smile on her face.

I feel Cameron's eyes on me as we enter, and I don't have to pretend to be impressed or delighted with what I'm seeing.

"This place is amazing."

Cameron beams. "Right? I'd totally eat here even if my mom didn't own the place."

As if on cue, the kitchen door swings open, and a small Asian woman steps out. Her dark hair is in a loose bun, and she wears a white apron over a light-blue blouse and jeans. She looks like she's around my dad's age, maybe in her early forties, and the smile that splits her face when she catches sight of Cameron leaves no doubt in my mind she's his mom.

"My darling boy, here on time for once!" she cries as she wraps her arms around him.

Cameron laughs and returns the hug. It's like

17

watching a cat get hugged by a panda—his mom almost disappears in the embrace.

"And you've brought a friend?"

Her dark eyes turn curiously to me, and I manage a polite smile.

"Hi, yeah, I'm Jasper."

"He and his dad just moved here," Cameron says, "and we got paired together for an English assignment."

All of which is true, but none of which is the real reason we're here. I didn't expect Cameron to be so good at sidestepping the truth, but turns out he's a pro.

"Say no more," his mom says. "We can set you up at the back table. It's the quietest one," she tells me with a conspiratorial nod. "Get your assignment finished, and you can help me out after you're done, Cammy. Do you like red bean?"

This last question is directed at me, and I sputter for a second. "I think so? I haven't really had much of it."

She pats my shoulder with so much enthusiasm it stings a little. "Don't worry, you'll love it. I'll bring over a few treats for you boys to munch on while you're working. And some bubble tea. Are you allergic to anything?"

"Um, no, just dust."

Her eyes narrow. "There is no dust in here, young man. I keep a clean establishment."

"No, I know, I didn't mean—"

She bursts out laughing, and Cameron joins her.

"Anyway, go have a seat, and I'll bring your food and drinks over when they're ready."

While I'm still blinking at her, Cameron takes my arm and leads me to the promised table in the corner. There are a few other people in the café, some college students and an old man reading a Korean newspaper, but none of them glance at us as we settle in opposite each other at the far table.

Cameron pushes the ceramic sugar packet holder to one side of the table. "Sorry about my mom. She can be kind of a lot sometimes."

"No, she seems great," I say. "And this place really is fantastic."

"Mom's only had it for a few years, but it's always been her dream. Anyway, I'll go get our drinks and stuff so she doesn't have to bring them over. Don't go anywhere, okay?"

I have no plans of going anywhere, and I'm more than content to sit and enjoy the ambiance of the shop while Cameron fetches our stuff from his mom. I hear them talking and laughing together and feel a moment's pang I was never that close to my own mom, or that she never let me be that close to her. But that's angst for another day.

The red bean buns, as it turns out, are just as delicious as Cameron promised, and the bubble tea may be an actual gift from above.

"Oh my God," I sigh after I take another sip. "How is it even legal for something to be this good?"

Cameron's smile is so wide his cheeks probably hurt. "Right? My mom's a freaking genius."

We munch and sip in silence for a few moments, and then Cameron folds his big hands on the table and meets my eyes.

"So I do want to say that even though we came here to talk about a certain thing you said today, we absolutely don't have to if you've changed your mind. I don't want you to feel pressured or anything."

I take a deep breath. "No, I want to talk about it. I've never told anyone about it before, and I think I'd kind of like to." I wince. "Though you might not like me too much after I tell you."

"Well, that's not gonna happen." He says it with a dismissive wave of his hand, like I'm speaking actual nonsense. "I liked you the second I saw you, and I'm pretty much never wrong about people."

I sit in stunned silence and wonder what it would be like to be Cameron, open and easy and friendly with everyone.

"Even so," I say, "I did some stuff I'm not proud of…"

"Hasn't everyone?"

"And I don't come out of this tale looking good, believe me. Felix is the victim in this story."

Cameron leans forward and clasps his hands under his chin. "Well, now you have to tell me."

I laugh. "I thought you didn't want to pressure me?"

"You've intrigued me too much, and now I must know! But seriously, you don't have to tell me if you don't want to. But I hope you will because I'm super curious."

I sigh and launch into the whole sordid tale. As I talk, the destruction of my friendship with Felix plays through my mind like a movie, as if it happened to someone else. Sometimes I wish it had.

Two boys sit together on a playground. They've been best friends forever, which is to say they met the previous September on the first day of school. They talk, laugh, play video games, have sleepovers at each other's houses, and spend every available second together.

It's a beautiful May afternoon, and they're lounging

on the grass behind the school swing set, spending their recess plucking dandelions from the ground and throwing them at each other. This turns into playful wrestling, and somehow they end up with one boy beneath, one boy above, their faces an inch apart. The one on top hesitates, then ducks down and presses his lips to the other boy's, sweetly and quickly.

Everything goes still. There's blank astonishment on the lower kid's face, but a smile pulls at his lips. He's just opening his mouth to say something when an eruption of sound jolts the two boys apart.

A girl stands behind them, pointing and making a disgusted face. "Ew, he kissed him!"

Other voices sound, other faces appear, and there are pointing fingers and laughter, a group converging to stare and mock. The boy who kissed his friend watches this transpire with gentle confusion on his face, but the boy who was kissed backs away and contorts his own face to match the onlookers.

"Yeah, gross!" he says, even though it wasn't gross at all.

The boy who kissed him stares at him, and something dies in his eyes.

They don't talk or even look at each other for the rest of recess, and there are no more sleepovers after that, and no more sitting next to each other or being best friends or any kind of friends at all. The boy who kissed gets laughed at more often, and shoved sometimes, and eventually it gets bad enough that his parents decide to move him to another school, far away from the laughter of the bullies and the accusing eyes of the boy he kissed.

Cameron doesn't interrupt me once as I talk. He listens quietly, sipping his bubble tea, and when I'm done, the silence stretches, and I wonder if I've lost the first friend I've made here.

"Well," he says at last, "you're right that what you did wasn't the best. But you learned from it, right?"

"Yeah…"

"Then that's all that matters."

The ease of his acceptance stuns me, and I fight to find my voice.

"I don't think it's that simple. I ruined Felix's *life*."

"Nah."

"He had to change schools, and now he's a raging homophobe. You don't think that had anything to do what happened back then?"

Cameron chews thoughtfully on his straw. "I mean, *maybe*. But not every queer kid who gets bullied turns into a homophobic prick, you know. I didn't."

I almost choke on my bubble tea, both because of how casually he's dropped that he is not, in fact, part of the straight ally faction of the QSA and because I'm trying to imagine anyone bullying him. "You got bullied?"

"When I was younger, yeah. Most of it stopped once I hit my growth spurt, but it was pretty bad for a while. My point is that just because a queer kid gets bullied doesn't mean they turn into a jerk because of it. So even though what you did to Felix wasn't great, I don't think you can take the blame for the person he's become since then."

I take another sip of my bubble tea. It's still nirvana in a cup. "How are you this wise?"

Another sunbeam of a smile from Cameron. "I am an old soul," he says with a dignified lift of his chin. "Anyway, it's obvious. You would've gotten there in the end."

I sigh and drop my head into my hands. "So what do I do?"

"About Felix?"

"Yeah. I still want to apologize to him, and maybe if I do, it'll, I don't know, snap him out of this internalized homophobia thing he's got going on and turn him into a decent person again."

Cameron kindly does not point out all the flaws in this plan. "What was he like when you knew him?"

I shake my head. Words don't seem like enough to describe it. "He was the best. Kind of quiet, but he never said a mean word to anybody, and he'd help out anyone who needed it. Which was usually me. He was so smart, too. They wanted to skip him ahead a grade, but he told his parents he didn't want to because he wanted us to still be in the same grade together."

Cameron snaps his fingers. "That explains it. I was wondering how you guys were in the same class back then, and I didn't want to ask awkward questions in case you got held back a year or something."

My stomach sinks a little. "You mean he's not in our grade?"

" 'Fraid not. He's a senior."

Which explains why I didn't see him in any of my classes today. He's a senior, which means he'll be graduating in June, and after that he'll be off to college somewhere, and I'll probably never see him again.

"I have to talk to him," I say, so fiercely that Cameron puts down his bean bun to stare at me. "I have to apologize and help him through this. He needs to know that what happened was my fault, not his, and that he doesn't have to be like this anymore. I know if I can just talk to him, he can get past this."

I expect Cameron to try to talk me out of it, but he just nods. "Okay. I'll help you."

"What?"

"I'll help. Whatever you need. And I might have an idea about how you can talk to Felix."

"You do? What is it?"

He flashes a mysterious smile. "All in good time."

We actually finish our English assignment after that, which is good since Ms. Keeley wants us to turn them in first thing tomorrow morning. After that's done, Cameron gets permission from his mom to further delay his café duties to walk me home. I dropped the clunker off before coming here, since the café's only a fifteen-minute walk from our house, and for all that I've spent the entire day with Cameron, I don't at all mind having him walking beside me as I navigate the streets leading home.

"Pop quiz," he says as we turn onto a street that leaves us squinting into the setting sun. "Pirate or astronaut?"

I glance at him. "Huh?"

"Which one did you want to be when you were a kid?"

"Oh. Astronaut, I guess. You?"

"Yar," he says, and I snort.

"Really? You don't want to go to space?"

"Nah, it makes me think of the ocean, no air and creepy things floating around."

"You know pirates literally sail on the ocean, right?"

"Details, arr. Anyway, at least with the ocean, you can sit on top of it in your boat. In space, it's all around you, no escape. But you do have a point. Maybe I should be a land pirate instead."

"So just a regular old criminal, then?"

"But with an eyepatch and a surly crew."

"Right. So why don't you like the ocean?"

He shudders. "I'm not a big fan of bodies of water. Ponds, lakes, but especially the ocean. I mean, anything could be down there. Sharks, jellyfish, Elvis..."

"Elvis? You think Elvis is in the ocean?"

"You don't see him on land anywhere, do you?"

He holds the serious expression for an impressive count of five before laughing, and I join him. It feels good. This whole day has felt good, and I know the reason for it is the guy walking beside me.

"It's weird," I say.

"What, Elvis in the ocean? I know, that was kind of the point."

"No, not that. I mean, *that*, but also that's not what I meant."

"Oh. What's weird, then?"

"This. You. I've never really had friends at school, not since Felix. And I guess I didn't think that would change. I hoped I could get Felix to like me again, but I didn't think I'd meet anyone else I liked, or that they'd like me, too."

"So you like me, then?" Cameron sounds pleased, and it fills my chest with warmth.

"I mean, yeah. Are there actually people out there who don't like you?"

His lips twitch upward. "Believe me, there definitely are."

"It's hard to imagine. You're really...likable."

"Well, thanks. I think you're pretty likable, too."

It dawns on me that Cameron is a guy who's into

25

guys, and I am also a guy who's into guys, and we both like each other and have had a frankly amazing day together, and now we're walking side by side into the sunset after an intimate study date at his mom's café.

A nervous tingle runs through me, but it fades the second I look into Cameron's open, smiling face. He is, after all, just an overall friendly person, and from everything I've seen of him today, it seems as if he likes pretty much everybody, and pretty much everybody likes him back.

Besides, my heart and mind are still very much fixed on Felix, and hopefully with Cameron's help, I can figure out how to reach the sweet, shy kid who once liked me enough to kiss me.

And after that, if he wants to kiss me again? I'm pretty sure I'll let him.

Chapter Four

I throw Cameron a skeptical look through my bedroom mirror as I adjust my tie. "I still can't believe you want me to do this."

His hands rest comfortably in the pockets of his khakis, and a blue tie covered in little cartoon donuts trails down the front of his white button-down. "It's a good idea."

"Church," I say doubtfully.

"Felix's church. And also my mom's church, which is how I know he goes there. And bonus, she's not going to be there today, so we can safely nap through the sermon without getting an elbow in the ribs."

"So we're just going to rock up to this church, two gay guys, and go have a chat with Felix. In a *church*."

Cameron rests his hand on my shoulder, the warm, steady weight of his palm pressing into my skin through my dress shirt.

"First of all, I'm pansexual," he says with an amused quirk of an eyebrow. "Well, panromantic demisexual, technically. And second, this is the only time you'll have any chance of catching Felix without his friends. At school, he's always around the other guys from the soccer team, and no way is he going to open up to you with them around. At church, though, it's just him and his parents, and when his parents go off to chat with their friends after the service, *bam*. You strike."

"And when we're chased out of the place by a torch mob of angry Christians?"

Cameron's lips twitch. "That's not going to happen. For one thing, I don't think they have any torches—"

"That you know of."

"—and for another thing, it's a pretty accepting congregation. I mean, my mom goes there. Do you really think she'd put up with any homophobic bullcrap?"

I've only met his mom the one time, but I already know she absolutely would not. No woman who would eat chicken nuggets in front of her crying children would put up with that kind of nonsense.

"I guess not," I say. "But I'm still…"

"What?"

"Nervous. I've never really felt comfortable in churches. My mom used to take me to one that had some pretty awful things to say about gay people, and I guess that kind of stuck with me."

"I promise, this church isn't like that. And if a bunch of homophobic pod people somehow took over the congregation since last Sunday, I promise we can leave right away."

"Right away?"

"At the first sign of a torch being lit, we're out of there. I promise."

I still don't feel great about it, but Cameron's right that this isn't a conversation I can have with Felix in front of his friends. I've only been at school for a week, and I already know it's safest to avoid them. They're gods of the school, and I've spotted more than one teacher looking the other way when it comes to them bullying people. Luckily, I haven't seen Felix being an active part of the bullying—he mainly just hangs back and watches—but the Felix I knew would never have done even that.

I give myself one last dubious look in the mirror but finally concede I look as church-presentable as it's possible for a nervous gay boy to look. When I turn around, Cameron is studying my bulletin board.

"Have you been to all these places?" He nods at my collection of European postcards.

"Most of them. Since Mom's from Spain, we've been there a few times to visit her family, and Dad convinced her to let us stop by some other places while we were there. We didn't get to stay long, but I made sure to grab a postcard at all the interesting spots."

Cameron's gaze shifts from my postcards to the collection of travel books and memoirs that line my bookshelf. "So is this your thing, then?"

"My thing?"

"The thing you're into. Like, I'm really into old movies and animation, and my sister loves animals. My mom's into baking and being a badass, and I guess some people are into sports or photography or art or…"

"I think I get the idea," I say with a smiling roll of my eyes. "Yeah, I guess it's my thing. I've just always been really interested in traveling to different places. Learning about new cultures, trying the food, learning about the history, stuff like that. I always wanted to do study abroad or something, but I figure I'll settle for trying to get accepted to a college in England or France or something."

"Not Spain?"

My jaw tightens. "Not Spain."

When I don't say anything more, Cameron turns away from my books. "Well, should we get going?"

We head downstairs, where Dad waits with a stack of pancakes. It's been ages since I've had a friend over, and Dad is practically vibrating with excitement at the presence of a real, honest to goodness classmate of mine standing in our kitchen.

Cameron, predictably, seems to love the attention, and to love my dad, as well.

"Oh my God, did you make all of this for us?" he demands as Dad lowers the pancakes onto the table. There are also eggs, veggie bacon, toast, jam, and fruit, and I can smell the rich scent of coffee brewing from across the room.

"This is *amazing,*" Cameron says. "My mom is always too tired to cook on the weekends, so I'm usually stuck with cereal or something for breakfast. This is fantastic."

Dad is positively glowing, and I know Cameron's made another friend for life.

"I've just always enjoyed cooking." Dad slides into his chair at the head of the table and beams at Cameron across the sea of mouthwatering breakfast items. "And it's a good way to relax. Even if this one doesn't eat enough of what I make."

Cameron shovels a massive chunk of pancake into his mouth, chews, and swallows. "Well, if you ever need any help eating anything, just let me know. That's one thing I'm always up for."

I have a flash of Cameron showing up every weekend for breakfast and feel warm all over. The whole house seems brighter with him in it, and even Dad seems happier, humming a little as he pours out three cups of coffee.

"How do you take it, Cameron?"

"Milk and three sugars." Cameron winks at me. "I like it sweet."

"Perfectly okay," Dad says.

I throw him a shocked look. "This from the same man who told me it was an actual, legally actionable crime when I put a single sugar into a cup of black coffee?"

"That's different," Dad says. "Cameron is a guest, and he can have his coffee however he wants. You, however, are my son, and I expect you to uphold certain universal truths, like the fact that black is the only proper way to drink coffee."

Cameron glances between us and barks out a laugh. "You two are the best." He stretches across the table to pat my hand, and warmth burns up my arm. "But I'm on Jasper's side on this one, Mr. S. Coffee's just so much better sweet."

Dad gives an easy smile. "You're young, so I'll forgive your blasphemy."

The rest of the meal is pretty lively, Dad and Cameron effortlessly falling into conversation while I mostly just eat my food and enjoy the show. The next fundamental thing they disagree on involves some board game I've never heard of, and because I have zero knowledge of the subject, I tune out in favor of sneaking looks at Cameron as he talks. He still looks completely relaxed, calm and friendly even in the presence of an adult he's just met. As always, his expression is open, hiding nothing, an easy mirror to everything that lies inside.

When the last drops of syrup have been mopped up, Cameron gathers his plate and mine and takes them to the dishwasher without being asked.

"We should probably get going," he says with a glance at his watch. "We don't want to be *too* fashionably late."

"Mm." Dad takes a solemn sip of his black coffee. "Wouldn't be fashionable."

I drain the last of my orange juice and give Dad the expected awkward sideways hug goodbye. "See you later."

"Drive safe. And don't come back religious. I taught you better than that."

He's teasing, but I still throw a glance at Cameron to make sure he's not offended. Dad and I are the agnostics of the family, and thankfully once I confided in him how much I hated going to church with Mom, he finally convinced her to stop taking me. Not that it really matters now, with her living in Barcelona with her boyfriend, but it was still a victory at the time.

Cameron doesn't look like he minds. He watches Dad and me with a warm smile, like everything is right with the world. Sometimes I wonder if everything *is* right with the world as far as he's concerned. I haven't known him for that long, but I've never seen him down or upset about anything. While I'm sure his life isn't all sunshine and rainbows, I can't help wondering what, if anything, gets under his skin.

Not, apparently, a freak September snowstorm, as he looks absolutely thrilled at the thick white flurries dancing through the air when we step outside.

"I'm not okay with this," I announce to the sky, huddling in my too-thin fall jacket because I refuse to wear my winter one on principle. "It was eighty-five degrees three days ago."

"Are you kidding?" Cameron tilts his head up and

laughs as big wet flakes slap him in the face. "This is amazing! It'll all be melted by tomorrow, so it's like a little sneak preview of winter."

"I don't need a sneak preview of winter."

"It's like a test drive. Take winter for a spin before you buy!"

"You're out of your mind."

"I'm an optimist."

"Same thing."

We pile into the car, and I try to dampen Cameron's enthusiasm for the snow by telling him he can scrape it off the windshield if he likes it so much. But of course, he takes the snow brush from my hands like it's a real treat and spends the next few minutes singing "Winter Wonderland" while he wipes snow off the car.

The heater has warmed the old clunker up a bit by the time Cameron hops back into the passenger seat, and we roll out of the driveway and onto the slush of the road. Visibility is pretty crap, but luckily Dad forced me to drive us everywhere in the snow last winter, and my seasonal driving instincts come back in a snap. Before long, I'm steering us down the snowy streets like a pro.

The church isn't too far away, but Cameron insists we have some sort of music to accompany us on our journey. Since the clunker doesn't even have a CD player—not that I own any CDs, but I'm sure Dad has some—I'm forced to listen as Cameron flicks the radio dial back and forth between stations, treating us to bursts of various genres until he settles on a polka station.

"You're joking," I say.

He blinks wide, innocent eyes at me. "My grandpa used to listen to polka. It's fun."

"It's making my ears bleed."

"That's part of the fun. Come on, who doesn't love accordion music?"

"Most sane people?"

"Well, you already said I'm out of my mind, so why not lean into it?"

I roll my eyes and fight a smile, but it's a losing battle. It's even harder when Cameron discovers he knows the song that's playing, and I listen to him singing in an enthusiastic, off-key voice about the dubious theft of a quiche or a keesh-ka or God knows what.

By the time we're nearly to the church, I catch myself nodding along to the latest accordion atrocity, and of course Cameron notices and grins so widely I have no choice but to switch off the radio and ignore him completely for a while.

The church parking lot is surprisingly full for a snowy Sunday, and choir music drifts to us from inside as we make our way to the front doors. It's more than a little weird being at a church again, and even though I know it's not the same one Mom used to drag me to, my whole body tenses as we draw closer to the entrance.

A hand wraps over mine, startlingly warm with the contrast of the frosty air.

"Hey." Cameron's voice is gentle, and his face is so close his breath whispers against my cheek. "I promise, it's going to be okay. No one's going to say anything to us. And if they do, I'll just sing polka music at them until they run away screaming."

I can't help but laugh at that, and Cameron grins like he's done exactly what he set out to do. The warmth slips from my fingers as he lets go of my hand, and we walk side by side into Felix's church.

Chapter Five

The last time I was at church was last Christmas, a week before Mom left. Despite Dad and me being pretty vocal about our lack of interest in anything church-related, she managed to talk us into going by promising homemade cinnamon buns after the service. As Dad rarely got to eat anything he didn't cook himself, this definitely interested him, and I've always been a sucker for a sticky, hot cinnamon bun fresh from the oven. So we went.

And honestly, it wasn't the worst. The Christmas service at least had familiar tunes, a familiar story, and no reason for the priest to bring up queer people and whether or not they might have a future burning in Hell.

And somehow, it still all went south.

It was just after the service, and Mom was chatting with a bunch of church ladies in fancy hats while Dad and I hung back by the wall with our arms crossed, avoiding people's eyes. I noticed Mom's gaze tracking over to me every now and then, and I was about to ask Dad about it when the priest himself appeared in front of us, smiling with his mouth but not his eyes.

"Well, the prodigal sons return!"

"Father James," Dad said. He hesitated before adding, "Good to see you."

I'd never liked Father James. He smiled a lot, but there was something dangerous lurking beneath it, like a predator about to strike. He wasn't that old, probably around forty-five—he still had a full head of neatly trimmed light-brown hair—but he carried himself like he was the oldest and wisest guy in the room.

"And young Jasper," he said. Like he was eighty and I was eight. "I'm glad to see you return to us, if only for the Christmas service." His eyes narrowed, and the back of my neck prickled with the unmistakable prey sense of *danger, danger.* "I've been wanting to speak to you, actually. I've heard some things about you that I'm hoping are not true, but one never knows, does one?"

While my brain was saying, *Who even says 'one' like that anymore?* my mouth took control and asked, "What have you heard?"

To my horror, Father James rested his hand on my shoulder. It was too warm, too heavy, and his breath smelled like sour menthol as he leaned in. "Your mother's concerned about you, son. She's spoken to me about you more than once, and each time, I can tell she's more concerned. She doesn't want you to be led astray."

I exchanged an uneasy look with Dad. Mom was laughing with her church lady friends, but I caught her glancing in my direction again and felt a cold twist of betrayal.

"How would I be led astray?" I asked.

Father James leaned close enough that I could see the bloodshot veins in the whites of his blue eyes. "By falling to *unnatural* desires."

Blood rushed in my ears, and I told myself he didn't mean what I thought he did. He couldn't. *She wouldn't…*

"It's normal to be tempted." He had finally lifted his hand from my shoulder, but he still stood way too close for my liking. "It's part of being human. But what sets the righteous apart from the unrighteous is that we-do-not-yield-to-temptation!"

Each word was punctuated by his fist slapping into his open palm. I wanted to throw up.

"So the next time you're sitting at your computer and thinking about looking at things that might inspire you to go down a dark and sinful path, think about our Lord and resist. Think about your mother, who loves you and wants you to live a righteous life. And think about what's waiting for you if you go down the wrong path. Is it really worth risking eternity in hellfire for a few minutes of satisfaction?"

My face was burning, and my chest felt like it was actually, literally on fire. I wanted to run, but my feet were rooted to the floor.

A strong arm slid around my shoulders, and Dad gave Father James a gentle but firm push backward, away from us, away from me.

"I think you've said enough." Dad's voice was low, angrier than I'd ever heard it. "We're leaving."

Father James called something after us, but the roaring in my ears drowned him out. Dad's arm never left my shoulders as he ushered me out of the church, down the front steps, and back to the car.

I slid into the passenger seat even though I knew I'd have to move when Mom came out. Dad dropped into the driver's seat, hesitated, and then locked the doors.

There was a long silence.

"If there's anything you want to tell me," he said softly.

"I'm gay," I blurted.

It wasn't how I'd planned to come out to him, but he'd probably already figured it out thanks to what

Father James had said. And between my parents, Dad was the one I knew would be okay with it.

"I wasn't looking at anything bad." The words spilled out faster and faster, tripping over each other. "I was just looking up ways to come out to people and watching some videos about things like that. I guess I forgot to delete my browser history and Mom found it." Heat rushed through me again, and I fought another violent urge to be sick. "And then she told Father James."

Dad's face was stony. "She had no right to do that."

"Go into my browser history, or tell Father James?"

"Either." To my surprise, he twisted the key in the ignition and started the car.

"What about Mom?"

He slid the car into drive. "It's only a few miles, and it's a nice day out. She can take the bus."

****

The singing is still going on as Cameron and I look around for a place to sit. It's not a big church, and most of the seats are already occupied, but we find an empty pew in the back row, way over in the corner. Cameron lets me slide in first, and that leaves me with the wall on one side and Cameron on the other, as if he's making a barrier between me and everyone else in the church. It makes me feel oddly protected, and I wonder if he has any idea how much safer I feel with his big, friendly self between me and the rest of the congregation.

Knowing him, he probably does.

I scan the rows but don't spot Felix right away, and before I can spiral too deeply into thoughts of, *What if he didn't even come today? What if we came here for nothing?* Cameron squeezes my hand, and the worried voice in the back of my mind goes quiet. It's hard to be anxious with him here beside me, so calm and sure and steady. I have a fleeting thought that maybe this won't be such an awful experience after all, but then the choir finishes their song to polite applause, and the minister steps up to the podium.

I steel myself for the worst.

Except the minister isn't some stone-faced old white guy ready to rain fire and brimstone on the congregation. She's a short Middle Eastern woman with only a hint of gray in her thick black hair, and she beams out at us like she knows Cameron is here and wants to give him some competition.

"Welcome, everyone." Her voice is warm and friendly, and despite the suspicion still prickling inside me, I relax a little. "First, let me thank you for coming out on this very snowy day. God works in mysterious ways, and the weather is definitely one of them!"

Laughter. I glance around the congregation and don't see a faceless sea of people who hate people like me. Instead, I see mothers, fathers, grandparents, kids, teens, and a lot of smiling faces.

"First, a few announcements. The youth club's softball game will not be held after services today, for obvious reasons." A gesture at the snow-splotched window is followed by more chuckles from the pews. "The women's Bible club meeting tonight is still on, though I'd advise dressing warmly since the heater in the meeting room hasn't been fixed yet."

To my astonishment, a voice from the crowd shouts, "Thanks a lot, Joe!"

An older man in the front row gets to his feet and yells jovially back. "It's the beginning of September! I figured I had at least a few weeks before we'd need the heater fixed!"

More laughter, and Joe sits down with a "harrumph" that's spoiled by the smile on his face.

"Finally," the minister says, raising her arms until the congregation settles down, "we'd like to offer our congratulations to two members of our church family, Matthew Harris and Jonathan Sanchez, who exchanged their wedding vows yesterday in a small ceremony at their home."

Two grinning young men stand up, holding hands, and nod their thanks to the minister while the congregation erupts in applause. My stomach turns a somersault.

"I was lucky enough to preside over the wedding," the minister continues, "and it was a beautiful ceremony, even if I'm a little disappointed I only got to have one piece of cake."

There are some laughing protests from the grooms, but I barely hear them. I turn to Cameron, my eyes wide.

"See?" he whispers. "I told you."

I'm too stunned to answer. I always knew in theory that not all churches were like the one my mom used to drag me to, but I never imagined something like this, where the actual minister would be celebrating a gay wedding while the congregation smiled and clapped.

I scan the crowd again, looking for the inevitable signs of disapproval from someone in the group, but I don't find any. What I do find is Felix. He's sitting a few rows up and to the left with his arms folded, looking bored—but at least not disgusted—while his parents smile and clap along with everyone else.

Which, honestly, throws me for a loop. I figured Felix's homophobia was coming from his parents or his church or something like that. I thought maybe his mom and dad were anti-queer and that was why he was pushing away that side of himself, or he was getting nasty messages from his minister like I'd always gotten from Father James. But it's starting to look like none of those things are true.

As the sermon gets going, I glance at Cameron to see if he's any more interested in it than I am, and to my surprise, he's dozing with his head drooping and a little drool trickling out of the side of his mouth.

Some people look different when they sleep, more relaxed or peaceful, but Cameron looks pretty much the same. His cheeks are a little flushed, and I notice he has really thick eyelashes, more visible now that they're fanned out against his cheek. Freckles dust the bridge of his nose, and his parted lips make way for soft, sleeping breaths. Looking at him, I'm possessed by a strange urge to brush the hair out of his face, or maybe just take him home and wrap him up in blankets so he can sleep this off somewhere more comfortable.

My neck prickles with the feeling of being watched, and when I tear my eyes away from Cameron, Felix is looking straight at me, his eyes dark and accusing. His eyebrows slash downward, and his lip curls as he stares at me. In this moment, he doesn't look anything like the Felix I used to know, and all I can do is stare back with wide eyes until he shakes his head and faces front again.

Cameron wakes up at the end of the service, gives a massive yawn, and wipes the drool from the corner of his mouth.

"Well." He stretches his arms over his head shamelessly as we shuffle out of the pew. "Ready to do this?"

Dread twists in my stomach, but I nod. Most of the congregation are on their feet and wandering around, some chatting with each other while others make their way down the aisle to the exit. I peer through the crowd just in time to see Felix slip through a door at the back of the church and into the hallway beyond.

Cameron gives my shoulder an encouraging nudge. "Go on, go after him. I'll be right behind you."

I weave through the friendly crush of bodies as best I can. A glance over my shoulder shows Cameron having a bit more trouble due to his size and the fact that he's stopped every few steps by someone wanting to hug him or pinch his cheek or ask how school is going. Even my anxiety about Felix doesn't stop me from finding that really freaking cute.

The back door takes me to a drafty corridor and an exterior door propped open by a hymnal. I hesitate with my hand on the doorknob for a small eternity, and then I step outside.

Felix is a few feet away, fumbling to light a cigarette. The snow has finally stopped, but the wind keeps blowing out his lighter until he turns his back, cups his hands, and manages to keep the flame going long enough to persuade the cigarette to light. He's probably cold wearing just his white dress shirt, black pants, and dress shoes, but he doesn't give any indication the icy air bothers him.

As if he senses me watching him, his gaze lifts and meets mine.

We live in that frozen moment for an instant or an eternity, and then I crunch across the snowy sidewalk and join him against the wall of the church. He eyes me warily but doesn't run away, pressing his back to the stone as he takes a long pull on his cigarette. Smoke puffs out of his mouth and into the frosty air between us.

"What are you doing here?"

They're the first words he's spoken to me since we were ten years old, and they're not friendly. His voice sounds older, deeper, but I still hear a hint of the old Felix in it. I hope I'm not imagining it.

"I wanted to talk to you," I say.

He exhales a breath that might be a laugh. "Why?"

I open my mouth to answer, but a question blurts out instead. "Since when do you smoke?"

He shrugs and takes another drag.

I take a tentative step closer to him. "Look, the truth is—"

"If you're here to apologize, you can save it."

The words I've rehearsed a thousand times dry up on my tongue.

"You were right back then," he says. "I don't know why I even did that. If you'd done it to me, I'd have been grossed out, too."

The words are all wrong, and I know they can't be true. Can they?

"No," I manage. "I wasn't grossed out. That's the thing, I wasn't grossed out at all, but everybody was looking at us and laughing, and I just panicked. I've felt awful about it all this time, and I just wanted to tell you that you didn't do anything wrong." I risk taking a step closer. "I *liked* it. I wanted you to kiss me. I was so glad when you did."

If I'm hoping for these words to magically transform the sour-faced smoker in front of me into the boy I used to know, I'm sorely disappointed. Felix casts me a dark look and tosses his cigarette into the snow.

43

"Better watch who you say that around. There are a lot of people who'd beat you up for less."

"And what about you? Are you going to beat me up because I liked it when you kissed me?"

His cheeks flush, anger and fear warring in his eyes. "If you say a word about that to anybody…"

A deep cold sinks into my bones that has nothing to do with the wintry weather. "God, Felix, what happened to you?"

"What do you mean?"

"I mean, this isn't you. You were the nicest person I knew, and now you're, what, some homophobic jock bully? What happened?"

He crushes the cigarette butt under his foot until it sizzles in the snow. "Look, don't talk to me at school. And you and your boyfriend better steer clear of my friends unless you want to get beaten up in the parking lot or something." He nods past my shoulder. "He looks like he can take it, but they'd break you like a twig."

I turn to find Cameron standing in the church doorway, serious and unsmiling. His eyes find mine, and the question in them is clear. *Are you okay?*

Before I manage more than a shaky nod, Felix turns on his heel and stalks off. A part of me says I should go after him, *make* him listen, but I just watch him go with a sinking feeling in my stomach. When Cameron puts his arm around me, I lean into him and rest my head on his shoulder.

"Come on," he says quietly. "Let's go."

Chapter Six

I flop onto my stomach on my bed, bury my head in my pillow, and groan. When I peel my face off the pillowcase, Cameron is sitting in my computer chair cradling his mug of tea and watching me with one brow raised.

"Better?" he asks.

I drop my face back into the pillow and groan again.

"Guess not," he says.

"Agh, it wasn't supposed to go like this!" I roll onto my back so I can glare up at the ceiling. "I'm not saying I expected him to accept my apology right away, but it's like he didn't even want it. He thinks I did the right thing pushing him away back then, and that's just so, so messed up. And he was smoking! He used to make anti-smoking posters and hang them up around the neighborhood, and he was *smoking!*"

"Definitely seems like he's changed a little since you knew him."

"Yeah, just a bit."

There's a pause as I study the ceiling, and Cameron drinks his tea.

"Do you like him?" Cameron asks.

I prop my head up on my hand. "What do you mean?"

He sips from his cup and doesn't meet my eyes. "I mean, you seem pretty caught up in helping him. And he kissed you way back when, and it sounds like you liked it. Were you hoping this would end in him kissing you again?"

I sigh and lie back. Cameron is just too freaking perceptive sometimes.

"Yeah, maybe?" I press my hand over my face. "I don't know. It's not like I thought it would be that easy, but I guess I figured if I could convince him to forgive me, we might pick things up where we left off."

"So the endgame here is for you and Felix to be together. As a couple."

He doesn't sound judgmental or doubtful or like this is a bizarre thing to want, so I nod. "Yeah, I guess. I mean, if he wants to. And if I want to. I definitely wanted to back then, but he's different now. We both are."

"Him more than you, it seems like."

"I still just don't understand how this happened. How could he have changed so much? And was it just because of what happened when we were kids, or did something else happen to him after? I just wish I could find out the truth."

"Well," Cameron says, "if that's what you want, then I guess we have to figure out how to get the two of you to spend some more time together. Maybe the more time you spend together, the more willing he'll be to open up to you."

I chew on my lower lip. It's a good idea, but... "What about you? Everybody likes you, and people spill their secrets to you all the time."

"Not all the time."

"Mr. Davies told you all about his divorce on Friday, and all you did was ask him to use the pencil sharpener."

He shrugs. "I guess I just have a face that makes

people want to tell me things."

"Exactly. So maybe if you get your face over to Felix, he'll tell you some things, too."

A slow breath of a sigh seeps through his lips. "I don't think that'll work."

"Why not?"

"Because I'm pretty sure that when he looks at me, all he sees is the chubby queer kid he and his friends used to bully."

I sit up so fast I almost knock a glass of water off my nightstand. "Felix used to bully you?"

Cameron runs his finger around the lip of his teacup, his eyes tracing the motion. "It was mostly the other guys, but yeah, he was in on it. Anyway, if he didn't fall for my charms back then, he probably won't now either, so it might be better if you try to talk to him instead."

"Oh my God, Cameron."

"I really wish you'd call me Cam."

"Fine. Oh my God, Cam. Have you seriously been spending all this time helping me figure out how to help someone who *bullied* you when you were younger?"

He shrugs, but I'm already on my feet and pacing.

"That's insane! If I'd known, I never would've asked you to help."

"I wanted to. And it's no big deal. It's in the past. I'm over it."

I throw him a doubtful look, but he just gives a mild smile in return.

"Honestly. I don't hold grudges. Life's a lot happier if you forget about things and move on."

I pace a few more steps and fold my arms. I don't know why I'm so angry about this, but I am. I'm furious.

"I just wish you'd told me. I've been such a jerk

about this…"

Cam pushes back his chair, and my pacing comes to a halt when he takes me by both arms and holds me still.

"Jasper." There's a soft affection I haven't heard in his voice before. "It's fine, I promise. It was a long time ago, and it honestly doesn't bother me anymore. Felix was a kid, and he did something stupid because everyone around him was doing it. Sound familiar?"

The fury bleeds out of me, and I sink where I stand. "I just don't like the idea of him hurting you."

And it's true. I'm furious about this because the thought of anyone hurting Cam really gets under my skin, but the thought of Felix hurting him makes me actually want to scream. Because if Felix hurt Cam, and Felix became the person he is now because of me, then Cam getting hurt is my fault.

"I wasn't a big fan of it when it happened, either. But it's over now. And even if it wasn't, that doesn't mean you should give up on Felix."

"You think so?"

"Of course. Everybody makes stupid mistakes, and everybody does dumb stuff because their friends are doing it. That doesn't make someone a bad person, and it doesn't mean you should give up on them." He hesitates. "Especially if you really like them."

Do I really like Felix? I did when we were kids, but I hardly know him now, and based on our conversation today, he's not too keen on reviving the friendship, let alone turning it into something more.

I drop onto the edge of my bed and loosen the tie I've just realized I'm still wearing. I don't know what happened to Felix between our kiss and now, but I do know deep in my gut that I'm at least partly responsible for how he's acting these days. And everyone he's bullied, every bit of misery he's caused... That's on me, too.

Determination fills my chest and makes me sit up straighter. "All right. Back to the plan, then. I need to figure out a way to spend more time with him."

Cam flops onto the bed beside me and slings his arm around my shoulder. "That, I think I can help you with."

****

Cam won't tell me his idea, but he asks me to trust him, and I do. Weeks go by, and despite the failure with Felix, I have to admit my life's never been better. Cam is in every class I have except Choir, and every morning he brings two red bean buns from his mom's shop while I bring a very hot, very sweet thermos of coffee for us to share. When Dad catches me dumping sugar into it one morning, he groans and staggers away like a wounded man, but I know he's joking. Mostly.

Cam helps me with math, which I'm abysmal at, and I help him with Spanish because Mom is a native speaker, and I have at least a basic understanding of the language from all the years of her yelling at me in it. Apparently I was pretty fluent when I was a little kid, but these days I struggle to conjugate my verbs just like my classmates.

We eat lunch with the kids from the QSA most days, and I find myself getting pretty close to Raven, who is funny and passionate and always shares her potato chips. I get along with a lot of the other QSA people, too, but any time something happens or someone says something funny or weird or completely insane, the first thing I want to do is tell Cam.

It's strange. I've lived my whole life up to now

without him, but suddenly everything I do is tied up in this one other person. He's the first person I talk to when I get to school and the last person I text before I go to sleep. Most days we hang out after school, sometimes at his mom's café and sometimes at my house. Dad wordlessly sets three plates around the dinner table anytime Cam is over, and even though Cam says more than once that we're under no obligation to feed him every time he comes by, I think Dad likes having someone to feed who happily devours everything he makes.

I see Felix sometimes in the halls, mostly when we both happen to be at our lockers at the same time. If his friends are with him, I keep my eyes safely trained away from him, but if he's alone, I offer him a little nod or a tentative smile and hope maybe this time he'll return it. He never does—his gaze scans past my face like I'm invisible—but I'm not too discouraged. It's hard to be down for very long when Cam is always there putting his arm around me or making me laugh about something, and I start to realize I might actually be happy.

Sometimes I think about that when I'm lying in bed at night. I stare up at the ceiling and feel the warm glow in the center of my chest and wonder if it's okay, if it's *right* for me to be happy when I caused Felix so much pain. I'm not sure I deserve to feel so good when he's still going around frowning in the halls and chain-smoking behind the bleachers, but I can't seem to help it. I'm happy.

And the reason is Cam.

Chapter Seven

Cam's idea comes to fruition the week before homecoming. It's the first week of October, and we're spending a rare Friday afternoon at the Matsumoto-Rogers household. Up until now we've avoided going there because Cam's mom apparently doesn't have much time to clean and has forbidden any guests while the house is less than spotless, but I've finally been granted a pass and am permitted to view the chaos.

"Honestly, this isn't even bad," I say as I slip my shoes off and follow Cam into the living room.

There are a few toys scattered here and there, a stack of magazines and schoolbooks on the coffee table, and a half-drunk glass of orange juice on the TV stand, but the place doesn't look messy, just lived in. I can't help flashing back to the way Mom always insisted our house be kept, spotless and artful and cold, a showroom instead of a home. There was a white sofa I wasn't even allowed to sit on, and I was never allowed to bring my toys out of my room in case I made a mess.

At Cam's house, though, there's a cozy brown couch that tries to swallow me up when I sit on it, and as I dig a little wooden train car out from underneath me, I feel immediately at home.

Cam flops onto the cushion next to me and stretches out his arms over the back of the couch. "Mom's a little bit of a perfectionist," he says, which gels with the woman I've been getting to know over the last few weeks. Yesterday I watched her take a perfectly good cat-shaped bean bun out of the display case because the tip of one of its ears was lopsided. "Luckily she never passed that onto me. You should see my room."

"Does that mean I actually get to see it?" I'm not sure why I'm so eager, but Cam's been in my room a dozen times, and I've never even had a glimpse of his.

Cam heaves himself off the couch and extends a hand to pull me to my feet. "Sure, if you want to. But I'm warning you, this is my mom's idea of messy, but my room? It is *messy*."

He's not exaggerating. I follow him up the stairs and down a short hall, and he opens the door to a full-on disaster area. Random clothing items litter the carpet, a set of dumbbells burrow dents into a pile of Cam's Spanish quizzes like aggressive paperweights, and an army of empty water glasses and tea-stained mugs crowd the nightstand. A plush blue comforter trails dangerously off the edge of the unmade bed, and the bookshelf is practically empty because most of the books are stacked on the desk, the dresser, the bed, or the floor.

"Well?" Cam spreads his arms wide as he surveys his kingdom. "What do you think?"

There's a corkboard on the far wall with a few medals and ribbons hanging on it, along with pictures of Cam and the QSA at some kind of festival, Cam and his family at the beach, and Cam as a chubby little kid in yellow overalls and a yellow bucket hat. A stuffed unicorn regards us cheerfully from the corner of the room, and the few posters on the walls are of old movies, mostly animated classics. Glow-in-the-dark stars speckle the ceiling, and the white walls gleam in the afternoon sunlight shining through the window. Everything is bright and chaotic and warm.

"It's very you," I say.

Cam beams like this is the highest compliment he could've received. "Honestly, this is the worst it's been in a while. I guess I haven't had much time to clean since we've been hanging out so much lately. But I'd pick you over a clean room any day."

Warmth floods through me while Cam grabs some clothes from the floor and shoves them into his closet like he's said nothing special at all.

He drags out two beanbag chairs, and I sink into the smaller orange one while Cam flops into the oversized yellow one and stretches out his arms and legs.

"So I guess we should get down to business," he says.

The beanbag beans rustle every time I move, and it's kind of soothing. "What business is that, exactly?"

"Operation Felix?"

That jolts me a little, because for all that Felix maintains a permanent residence in the back of my mind, I haven't actively been thinking about him much lately. The QSA is working on a ton of stuff for homecoming, and I've been caught up in that, and in my homework, and in finally convincing Cam that the car theft driving game we've been playing is more fun when you don't spend the whole time driving the speed limit and politely obeying traffic laws. I'd almost forgotten he was working on some grand plan to get Felix and me together.

I perk up and grant Cam my full attention. "So does that mean you're finally going to tell me your big plan?"

"It's not really a *big* plan, but it did take some doing.

I wasn't sure it would work out, which is why I didn't want to tell you before now, but… Well, it looks like it's a go."

I wait for him to go on, but he's clearly enjoying forcing me to wait in suspense. "Come on!" I smack his shoulder with the flat of my hand. "Tell me!"

Cam leans forward, his eyes sparkling. "So you know how there are all these different committees for homecoming?"

"Yeah…"

"Well, one of those committees is in charge of selling tickets for the dance. The actual selling is a two-person job, and all you have to do is sit there during the lunch periods next week and sell tickets to anyone who wants them. It's a good hour and a half of time together every single day, and since most people buy their tickets on the first day, for most of the week you'll just be sitting there with nothing to do but talk to each other."

The pieces fall into place in my head, and my mouth drops open.

"Are you telling me that me and *Felix* are going to be those two people?"

Cam just grins.

"How in the hell did you manage that?"

"The captains of the varsity sports teams always help out with homecoming. It's a tradition, so Felix was already going to be signing up for something. But I may have mentioned to a friend of mine on the student council that Felix would be the perfect choice for selling tickets since he's all good-looking and popular but also isn't the kind of guy who'd enjoy, say, picking out decorations for the dance or something. And so that friend convinced Felix to sign up for ticket sales, and I signed you up, and here we are."

I sink back against my beanbag. "You're amazing. Honestly, I can't believe you did that for me."

Cam's cheeks are a bit pink as he ducks his head. "It's not a big deal."

"Well, it is to me." I crawl out of my beanbag and wrap my arms as far as they'll go around his chest, burying my face in his shoulder. "Seriously, thank you. You're an amazing friend, and I really don't deserve you."

Cam doesn't hug me back right away, but then his arms come up around me and squeeze me tight for a second. "Yeah, no problem." His voice sounds a little strange, but it's probably just that I'm not used to hearing it from so close.

Hugging him feels really good, safe and comfortable and warm, but I force myself to move after a few seconds so I don't make things weird. I flop back onto my own beanbag, which seems colder and less comfortable now that I know the alternative.

"So." Cam's cheeks are still flushed, his gaze fixed on his fingers as they tap together in his lap. "Hopefully with all that time together this week, you'll be able to patch things up with Felix, or at least get started in that direction. And if things go really well, you can always sell yourselves tickets to the dance and go to it together."

I breathe out a skeptical laugh. "Let's not get ahead of ourselves. I don't know if he's even going to want to talk to me, let alone go to the dance with me."

"Hey, you never know."

An odd stretch of silence follows, and I clear my throat. "So are you planning to go to the dance with anybody?"

His eyes flicker up to meet mine before darting away. "Nah, probably not."

"Why not? You know, like, *everybody*, and pretty much everybody likes you. I bet you could get a date easy."

He shrugs. I expect him to say more on the subject, but instead, he hauls himself out of the beanbag and holds out a hand. I let him pull me to my feet.

"Come on," he says. He still holding my hand, but it barely registers. "We better stake our claim to the living room TV before Alice comes home, or we'll be stuck watching nature shows all afternoon."

The first time I met Cam's sister Alice was in passing at the café, but she definitely made an impression. Her bright blue shirt was covered in dolphins, her backpack was a shark, and the barrettes in her short black hair were otters. After saying hi to Cam and nodding shyly at me, she retreated to a corner table and spent the next hour poring over a nature magazine about blue whales, occasionally taking notes in a notebook with a family of clownfish on the cover. Apparently her dream is to become a marine biologist or some other wildlife-adjacent professional, and I have no doubt she would happily condemn us to five hours of the animal network if given the chance.

I follow Cam into the hall, and he doesn't let go of my hand until we reach the stairs and have to switch to single file. We spend the rest of the afternoon chilling on the couch with our feet up on the coffee table, watching movies and talking and gorging on snacks. When Alice peeks into the living room, Cam casually flips her over his shoulder and swings her around, making her squeal and nearly drop her shark backpack.

When he sets her down, she laughs and punches his shoulder, and he of course pretends to be mortally wounded and falls back onto the couch while clutching his arm, landing with his head pretty much in my lap. Once Alice heads to the kitchen with a laughing shake of her head, Cam grins up at me, and something possesses me to brush a silky black tuft of hair out of his eyes. He catches my hand midmotion, and suddenly we're sitting with his head in my lap, eyes locked, his fingers wrapped around mine. Even though I'm used to a certain amount of physical closeness in our friendship, this feels different, and my breath catches.

It's just for an instant, though, because then Cam sits up and offers me a chip from the chip bowl, and everything is back to normal.

Chapter Eight

When lunchtime on Monday rolls around, I'm half wondering if Felix will take one look at me and run the other way. And when he turns the corner and spots me manning one of the two chairs at the homecoming dance ticket table, he misses a step, and I swear there's actual panic in his eyes. But he covers it quickly, and soon he's back to being a bored, uncaring soccer god slouching toward me.

The ticket table is set up in the hallway outside the lunchroom, and when the bell rings for lunch in five minutes, we're probably going to be swamped. But for now, it's just Felix and me alone in the hallway, me watching his every move and him looking at everything except me.

He slumps into the metal folding chair next to mine and crosses his arms. "Did you arrange this somehow?"

"I didn't do a thing," I say. And it's the truth.

He scoffs in my direction and then shifts his attention to the table. There are stacks of tickets held together by rubber bands, a clipboard to take down names of attendees and how many tickets they've bought, a calculator for figuring out change—since we're not allowed to be on our phones—and a lockbox for the cash. It's all pretty straightforward, but since I got here first, I received the official rundown from the student council guy before he had to leave to do something else important and homecoming-related.

"It's pretty simple," I say, keeping my tone businesslike so as not to spook Felix any more. "They write down their names and info, they pay us the cash, we give them the tickets. And their change, if there's any."

Felix's voice is bone-dry. "Pretty sure I could've figured that out on my own."

"Probably. You always were about a thousand times smarter than me. Especially with math."

"Yeah, you should probably let me be the one to make change, or you'll end up giving half our profits away."

He smiles a little as he says it, and then he blinks and returns to the important business of glaring at the table.

"What are you even doing here?" he mutters.

I wave my hand at the crowded tabletop. "Selling tickets?"

"Not here at this table. Here at this school. How'd you even know I go here?"

Hope prickles through me. There's accusation in his tone, but there's curiosity, too.

"I didn't. I mean, not at first. Dad wanted to move after the divorce, get a fresh start, and this was the place he picked. I didn't even realize you went here until…"

This time, curiosity outweighs the hostility in his expression. "Until what?"

My voice softens as I remember sitting at my computer with hope and fear lancing through me like an electrical shock. "Dad had me browsing the school's website, and one page was about the varsity sports teams. It talked about how you'd been named captain this year.

And yeah, it could've been some other Felix Morales, but the second I saw it, I just knew. I knew it was you."

Felix is quiet for a long time. Then he gives a fractional nod and starts drumming his fingertips against his thighs.

"So why'd you start smoking?" I ask.

His drumming fingers freeze. "What?"

"You used to worry about getting lung cancer from your dad barbecuing on his grill. I just wondered how you went from that to a full-on nicotine fiend."

His lips twitch upward, just a fraction, before settling back into their standard frown. "Yeah, well, things change."

I let the silence stretch, and he shrugs uncomfortably.

"I don't know, I guess just 'cause all my friends do it. You don't want to be the only guy not smoking."

"Doesn't seem so bad if you're the only guy without lung cancer."

He rolls his eyes. "I think my lungs will be okay."

"That's not what your posters used to say." I clear my throat and raise a finger in classic oratory fashion. " 'Cigarettes stain your lungs with tar. Choose not to smoke and you'll go far.' "

Another twitch of Felix's lips, but he says nothing, so I continue.

" 'Cancer comes to those who smoke, steer clear of cigarettes or you will croak.' "

This time there's a snort of laughter, and Felix actually looks at me. I'm stunned all over again by the soft brown depths of his eyes, and it's amazing how much more he looks like my Felix when he's not scowling.

"How do you even remember all of that?" he asks.

"I have an ear for fine poetry."

"You have an ear for garbage, more like."

"How dare you. The writer of those lines was my very best friend."

The words drop heavily between us and lie there, and Felix turns away from me.

"Yeah, well," he says quietly. "Your best friend sounds like a big, embarrassing dork."

"He was," I say. "But so was I, so it was pretty okay."

I want to say more, launch into the next stage of my Felix friendship crusade, but the bell rings and suddenly the hallway is thick with noise and people. A line forms in front of our ticket table almost immediately, and our moment is over.

****

It takes about fifteen minutes for the line to dwindle, and then our potential ticket buyers shuffle off to eat their lunches in the cafeteria, and Felix and I are left alone again. Mr. Harrison, the student council advisor, dropped off some sandwiches, chips, and sodas for us during the ticket rush, and I reach for one of the sandwiches at the same time Felix does.

Our fingers brush, and Felix yanks his hand back like he's been burned.

"You go ahead," I say. "You always were a pickier eater than me."

He hesitates and then grabs the egg and cheese, and I take the hummus and veggie one and start to unwrap it.

"What do you even want?" Felix mutters as he picks the tomato slices and lettuce out of his sandwich.

"What do you mean?"

"I mean, why did you come after me at church? Why do you keep trying to talk to me? Do you want us to be best friends again or something? Because that's not gonna happen."

I take a bite of my sandwich and wash it down with a sip of orange soda. "I don't need us to be best friends again. I mainly just wanted to apologize to you because what I did was super crappy, and I've felt awful about it ever since it happened. But then when I saw how you were…"

His eyes narrow. "What do you mean, how I was? How am I?"

I set down my sandwich and face him. "It's like you're not even you anymore. You used to be the nicest kid I knew, and now… I just want to know what happened to you. And help you if I can."

His expression is closed and hard again, keeping me out. "You think I need help? You know I'm the captain of the varsity soccer team, right? And I have a 4.0 average? And I've already been accepted into a bunch of good schools? I'm popular, I have friends, I have a gorgeous girlfriend—"

"But you're not *you*." On a mad impulse, I reach across the table and rest my hand on his wrist. "This isn't you, Felix. Bullying people, doing stuff just because your friends are, acting like you don't care about anything or anybody. That's not the Felix I knew. The Felix I knew was a freaking amazing person who just cared so, so much about everything and everyone."

His gaze locks on my hand where it rests on his bare skin, and I see the moment when he decides to pull his arm away. "Yeah, well. That didn't work out too well for him, did it?"

"I just want to know what happened." Desperation breaks into my voice, but I'm way past caring. "Honestly. What happened to you? Was it because of me? Because of what happened back then?"

Felix stares down at the little pile of tomatoes next to his sandwich, a war behind his eyes. He takes a breath—

"'Ey, Morales!" booms a voice, and I turn to see three of Felix's friends from the soccer team swaggering toward us.

They shouldn't even be here—seniors have lunch next period, so they should be in class right now—but a lot of the teachers look the other way when the soccer team is involved, especially since there's a championship game in a few weeks.

Felix slaps hands or bumps knuckles with each of his friends in turn, scooting his chair away from mine as he does so.

I've never spoken to any of these guys before, but I know who they are. Everyone does.

Tyler is the golden boy, buff and blond with a chiseled jaw and annoyingly sultry blue-green eyes. The guy has a new girlfriend every other week, and I swear half the teachers are in love with him, too. Probably why he gets away with pretty much anything, and why he saunters around school like his mere presence is a gift to everyone he passes. We have Choir together, and yesterday he spent the whole period launching spitballs into Maria Rodrigo's hair while his buddies snickered.

Standing next to Tyler is Mac Yang, Felix's co-captain. Mac is skinny and spiky-haired and apparently runs like the freaking wind, if the wind scowled a lot and wore five-hundred-dollar sneakers. My main experience with him was a misguided moment in the first week of school when I reflexively picked up a pen he'd dropped in the hallway, and he snatched it out of my hand with a look of disgust that clearly said, "Hands off, loser."

The last guy, who everybody calls "Muncher" for reasons I don't want to investigate, is squat and short and has a perpetually nasty look on his face like something's died, and he's just started to smell it. He's the one I've had the fewest encounters with, and I'm kind of glad about that. I have nothing to go on but my own intuition, but I feel like he's the worst of the bunch.

It doesn't take long to realize I'm probably right about that. Before I can react, Muncher snatches my sandwich from the table and takes a huge bite out of it. And suddenly the nickname makes more sense.

"Mm," he says through a mouthful of bread, hummus, and roasted vegetables. "Thanks, man. I was starving."

He returns the mangled remains to me while the others laugh. Felix doesn't join them, his gaze lingering on my mutilated lunch.

"So what are you guys doing?" Felix asks.

"Ditching Chem." Tyler takes a long drag from my orange soda without even a glance in my direction, like I don't exist. He hands the can to Muncher before turning his attention back to Felix. "You stuck selling tickets all week?"

"Yeah." Felix's voice when he talks to his friends is monotone, flat and lifeless. "Every day except Friday, both lunches."

"Lame," Muncher says, only he belches it, because sure.

"You oughta come ditch with us," Tyler says. "We

were gonna go hang out behind the bleachers, grab a smoke."

Mac hasn't said much, and I wonder if he's not as bad as the rest of them after all, but then he grabs my bag of chips and upends it over Muncher's face while Muncher tries to catch the chips in his mouth. Soon the floor is littered with ruffled potato carnage.

Felix watches all of this without comment, then says, "Nah, I better stay here. Harrison said he'd be coming by to check on us."

Mr. Harrison said no such thing, but I keep my mouth shut.

"So?" Tyler folds his arms over his green and white varsity jacket. "Just have your little loser buddy here tell him you went to the bathroom or something."

I wait for Felix to refute our "buddy" status, but he just shrugs. "Nah, I better not. My mom's already on my case about getting in trouble so much. One more call from the school, and I'm grounded."

Muncher delights us with another belched, "Lame!"

But Tyler's face twists in wincing sympathy. "Yeah, my mom's like that, too. And we definitely don't want you getting grounded. Hailey'll kill you if you can't take her to the dance, and if Hailey's not happy, she's not gonna do anything to make *you* happy, if ya know what I mean."

Tyler, Mac, and Muncher break into nasty chortles, and I resist the urge to throw up the one bite of my sandwich I managed to get before Muncher got his hands on it.

A hint of weariness enters Felix's voice as he averts his eyes from his friends' leering faces. "Yeah. I guess."

The group exchanges a farewell series of hand slaps

and fist bumps, and after Tyler takes one more long pull from my soda, the soccer gods slouch off and leave us in peace.

I blink at the shattered remains of my lunch and then turn to Felix.

"You can't seriously tell me you like those guys."

Felix tears at his sandwich. "Shut up, they're my friends."

"They're not anybody's friends. They're, I don't know, cavemen. Neanderthals. What would happen if Bigfoot had babies with a really unintelligent rock."

That earns me a tiny breath of a laugh, but then Felix shakes his head again.

"It's none of your business who my friends are." He finishes whatever culinary surgery he was performing and, to my surprise, hands me half of his remaining sandwich. "Here."

I take it, eyes wide. "Thanks."

Felix grunts and goes back to eating what remains of his lunch, and I take a bite of sandwich unmarred by the saliva of Muncher.

****

Felix giving me half his lunch does not turn out to be the sign of a miraculous breakthrough between us. He spends the rest of our ticket-selling time frowning at his phone, which he's not even technically supposed to have out, and the few times I try to engage him in conversation, he either grunts or doesn't reply at all. When the bell rings at the end of Lunch B, he gathers up his sandwich wrapper, chip bag, and soda can and walks off without a word.

I breathe a deep sigh and do my own tidying, ignoring the chip debris Mac and Muncher left on the floor because screw that. I'm just grabbing the clipboard and the lockbox to return to Mr. Harrison when Cam shows up.

The sight of him is like a burst of sunshine after a day of gray, stormy weather. Even his clothes are like a sunburst—a bright yellow polo shirt paired with white pants dotted with yellow flowers. I'd look like an absolute tool if I tried wearing something like that, but on Cam, it works.

"Hey!" He relieves me of the lockbox and clipboard so I only have to carry my bookbag and lunchtime trash. "How'd it go?"

I sigh as we start toward Mr. Harrison's classroom. "Not awful? But also not great. We talked a little, but he still spent most of the time ignoring me, so I don't know. Also, his dumb friends showed up—"

"Did they say anything to you?" I'm not prepared for the intensity of Cam's stare or the dangerous undertone in his voice.

"Not really. They ate half my lunch, but Felix shared part of his sandwich with me after that, so it was okay."

Cam's eyes stay narrowed for a second longer, and then he pats me on the back with his free hand. "Well, hey, that's a good sign!"

"I guess."

"You don't sound too happy."

I'm not, and I probably should be. I got to spend a nice chunk of time with Felix today, and we made more progress on repairing our broken friendship than I'd thought possible. So why aren't I happier?

"I don't know," I say. "It's just a lot, I guess. Anyway, we'll see what happens tomorrow."

"And the day after, and the day after."

My lips bend into a small smile. "Yeah."

Cam wraps his arm around my shoulders, and I lean into the reassuring heat of his body. We walk the rest of the way to Mr. Harrison's room like that, and when Cam moves away from me to drop the lockbox off on Mr. H.'s desk, I miss the solid, steady warmth of him against me.

Chapter Nine

Raven taps her purple nails on the side of her soda can. Her opinion is pretty clear from the look on her face, but she offers me a diplomatic smile. "Well, what do you think?"

I sigh and drop my arms. "It's still not right, is it?"

We're in the drama department's costume room, and I've been trying on various colorful outfits for what feels like an eternity but has probably only been an hour.

"I didn't want to say it," she says with a lift of her sculpted eyebrows, "but yeah. Doesn't seem like the one."

She's lounging in a worn green armchair by the costume racks, flipping through papers on a clipboard while she assists me with my outfit hunt. She looks particularly artsy and cool today in a sparkly white tee under purple denim overalls that end in a skirt, paired with sheer black tights and her usual combat boots. I wonder, not for the first time, where exactly she shops.

At my dispirited expression, she gets to her feet and puts on the determined Raven face I've gotten so used to seeing during my time at the QSA. Her hands find my shoulders, and a laugh jolts out of me as she gives me a playful shake. "Jasper, we *will* find you something to wear on the float. And if it's not absolutely perfect, I'm pretty sure that'll be okay."

I slump where I stand. "I know. I know it probably

doesn't matter all that much, but this is my first time doing anything like this. I've never even really been 'out' before, and I just want to do it right."

Raven taps her knuckles against my arm. "There's no 'right' way to be out, ya dope. Being out just means being yourself, but in front of people." She fingers the hem of the tie-dyed blouse-like thing that's currently dwarfing my torso. "With that said, I don't think this is quite 'you.' "

"I'm starting to think nothing in this room is me."

"Buck up, kid. Cameron will be here soon with food, and I have a feeling that'll make everything seem brighter."

The reminder of our incoming taco delivery does lift my mood, but before I can comment, footsteps echo from the hallway, and a short girl with cropped red curls strides into the room.

The girl stops dead at the sight of us, and then she flashes Raven a crooked grin.

"Hey, fancy meeting you here."

"Uh yeah, Jess, hey!" Raven's voice comes out higher than usual, and she starts fidgeting with the strap of her overalls. "How, uh, why, uh… What are you doing here?" She winces. "Sorry, I didn't mean that to sound all accusing, like, *what are you doing here*, but… Yeah. What are you doing here?"

The girl—Jess, I brilliantly deduce—looks amused. She's wearing a black T-shirt with a giant orange cat face on the front, green cargo pants, and black boots not dissimilar to Raven's. A plaid flannel rings her waist, and she carries a worn pair of drumsticks.

"Just finished marching band practice, and I remembered I left one of my practice books down here."

She heads over to the chair Raven was sitting in and ducks behind it. When she straightens, she's holding a drumming practice pad and a slim white book with "Advanced Drum Techniques" printed across the front.

"I come down here to practice sometimes. This might surprise you, but the band room can get kind of noisy."

Raven barks out a too-loud laugh. "Ha, yeah, I bet, right. Totally."

Jess blinks and then hides a smiling cough behind her hand. "Well, I'll get out of your way. Good luck with whatever you're doing, and see you later, yeah?"

She's already out in the hallway when Raven calls after her, "Yeah, see you later!"

Once Jess's retreating footsteps have faded, Raven buries her face in her hands and mutters something that sounds like "stupid, stupid, stupid."

I press my lips together to hold back a smile. "Um, so what was that?"

Her hands drop from her face, and she picks up her clipboard and starts flipping through it at roughly the speed of light. "What do you mean?"

"Pretty sure you know what I mean."

The flipping stops, and she drops into the chair and groans. "All right, fine. I like Jess. She's amazing and wonderful and I want her to be my girlfriend. Happy?"

My eyebrows shoot upward, as I wasn't expecting quite this dramatic of a confession. "Wow, okay." I lower myself onto the armrest of the chair and poke Raven gently on the shoulder. "So have you told her how you feel?"

"Obviously not."

"Why not? Is she…" I wince. "I mean, I've never

71

seen her at the QSA. Is she straight?"

"She's a lesbian." Raven presses a hand over her eyes. "She doesn't come to QSA because she's busy with band, but she's definitely gay. That's kind of the problem."

"How exactly is that a problem?"

Her voice is soft, defeated. "Because I'm trans, Jasper. Some people are weird about that. I know I'm a girl, and a girl who likes girls should also like me, but sometimes it doesn't work out that way. And it's not like Jess has ever said anything transphobic, but you just never know."

It sounds like she's speaking from experience, and sympathy twists in my gut. "Well, maybe some people are like that, but Jess seems pretty cool. Maybe you should just, you know. Talk to her about it?"

Raven's gaze drops to the floor. "Would you lose respect for me if I told you I'm scared to do that?"

It's weird to see her so vulnerable. I'm used to the efficient, confident Vice President Raven striding around QSA meetings putting out fires and getting stuff done. It occurs to me for the first time that maybe she's confident and in control all the time because she has to be, because the best defense against homophobes and transphobes is to be so strong and comfortable with yourself that their insults can't touch you.

I'm not as good as Cam at being physical with people, but it feels right to rest my hand on Raven's shoulder and squeeze. "Of course I won't lose respect for you. If anything, stuff like this makes me respect you more. Here I was thinking you were some fearless, untouchable badass, but turns out you're scared of stuff just like the rest of us. And you *still* manage to be so awesome all the time."

Raven rolls her eyes, but she's smiling. "Laying it on a little thick there, Sinclair."

"I mean it, though. If you're not scared of anything, it's easy to be brave. But when you're terrified and you do something anyway? That takes guts."

Her arm snakes around my waist and squeezes. "You're a big ole sap, but you make some good points. I'll think about it. In the meantime, let's get back to the costume hunt, shall we? Otherwise we really will be here all night."

Before I can head wearily back to the racks in search of another outfit, Cam bounds into the room with two coffees and a bag that smells like delicious fried things.

I practically collapse in relief. "Oh thank God."

Cam grins as he lowers the coffees and take-out bag onto the table by the wall. "I wish everyone was that glad to see me."

Raven is already pawing at the bag. "I'm glad to see anyone who brings me tacos. Did you get the creamy jalapeño sauce?"

Cam produces a fistful of sauce packets from his jacket pocket. "Please, what do you take me for?"

Raven accepts them with upraised hands and stows them reverently in her own pockets. "Break for dinner?"

"Yes, please," I say.

"I'm gonna head up and see how everyone else is doing, but I'll be back in a bit, and we can get this wrapped up." She points a purple nail at my face. "Do *not* get any taco sauce on the costumes, or Ms. Shelby will murder us both."

I resist the urge to salute or say "yes, ma'am" and just nod. Raven shoots me one last stern smile and marches off with her dinner.

I collapse into her vacated chair. "I'm exhausted."

Cam tosses me a sympathetic wince as he pulls a feast's worth of tacos and sides out of the bag. "That bad?"

"I'm starting to deeply regret volunteering for this."

He drops a taco into my hand and drags over a metal folding chair. "What exactly were you expecting?"

"I don't know. I figured I'd tape some crepe paper onto the float or brainstorm theme ideas or something. I didn't think I'd be dancing on top of it."

"First of all, I already told you, you don't have to dance if you don't want to. You can just stand there and wave if that's more your style. Second, you won't be the only one. I'll be there, too, and so will a bunch of other people."

"Then why aren't you all having to suffer through hours of costume hell?"

"We're wearing the same things we did last year." He pats me on the head, smashing my curls down and then letting them spring back up. "Sorry, noob. This is the trial by fire we all have to endure. We did our time, and now you must, too."

I groan, but one bite of crunchy black bean deliciousness and the bad feelings melt away. Tacos always make things better. "Thanks for the food, by the way."

"Anytime." Cam unfolds a napkin and flaps it out into a cape, then tucks it into my shirt collar like a bib. When I blink at him, he drops his hand and takes a hurried step backward. "Er, Raven wasn't kidding about not getting sauce on the costumes."

We eat in comfortable silence, unbroken except for

the loud rustle of my napkin bib every time I move. At first, I ignore it in favor of focusing on my food, but finally I can't take it anymore. Tossing aside the crumpled wrapper of my first taco, I pull the shirt over my head and hunt around for where I left my sweatshirt. The costume room floor is littered with discarded outfits, so I don't spot it right away.

"Hey, Cam, have you seen—"

To my surprise, he's staring at me with wide eyes, jaw slack and taco forgotten in his hand. I swallow and fold my arms over my bare chest.

"Um, never mind, I think I see it."

I turn my back on him, my stomach suddenly all twisty and nervous. He doesn't say anything, and eventually I find my sweatshirt and pull it on over my head. Safely clothed again, I snag another taco from the table and drop back into my chair.

"So um." I glance around the room for inspiration and settle on a safe topic. "You looking forward to homecoming?"

"Mm," Cam says. He's paying a lot of attention to his taco, chewing every bite thoroughly. "You?"

"Yeah, I think so. I never really went to it at my old school, so yeah. Should be fun."

The silence that follows feels a little awkward. But it's been a long day, and I'm tired and itchy from trying on an endless parade of costumes, so I'm probably just imagining it.

And maybe I am, because Cam flashes me his usual smile as he crumples up his third taco wrapper. "So, I kind of have a suggestion for your costume, if you want to see it."

I sit up straight in my chair. "If it means I get out of

another hour of this hell, I will seriously wear anything."

Cam arches an eyebrow, and I feel my cheeks warming. But before I can sputter that I don't mean *anything*-anything, he's out of his chair and heading to the back of the costume room. I start to follow, but I've barely made it five steps before he's back.

"Ta-da." He holds out an outfit on a wooden hanger.

I stare. And stare some more.

It's gorgeous. It's a one-piece bell-bottom pantsuit comprised of mostly tassels and fringe, all rainbows and glitter with a dramatic plunging neckline. It looks like it belongs in a gay nightclub in the 1970s.

"Oh my God," I say.

"Apparently Ms. Shelby picked it up at a thrift store a few years ago when she thought they were doing some disco musical, but they ended up doing something else instead. This guy's been collecting dust ever since, which is honestly a crime. What do you think?"

I shake my head. "I love it. But I've never worn something like that in my life."

"Well, then you're overdue, aren't you?"

"It looks kind of tight, too, and... I don't know. What if I can't pull it off?"

Cam's lip twitches. "It has a zipper."

I try to glare at him but can't help laughing. "You know that's not what I mean."

He shakes the pantsuit at me, and a thousand tasseled rainbows erupt.

I heave a smiling sigh. "Okay, give it here."

Not wanting a repeat of the earlier weirdness, I make sure to go behind the folding screen at the back of the room to change. I have doubts the pantsuit will even fit me, but it goes on snugly but not uncomfortably, and soon I'm staring at my reflection in the mirror and wondering where Jasper Sinclair went.

"Well?" Cam calls. "How is it?"

"It's, um." I give my body a little shake, and the glittery rainbow tassels dance around me. "I think it's…good?"

I step out from behind the screen and hold my arms out so Cam can see the whole outfit.

His eyes widen when he catches sight of me, and the smile that comes to his face makes me feel a confusing combination of pleased and self-conscious.

"Wow," he says. "You look… Really great."

I glance down at myself. The neckline dips almost to my stomach, leaving a bare strip of chest that probably needs some '70s-style gold chains or something to complete it, and the whole outfit is snug, hugging my body in a way I'm not used to. "Do I? Because I feel like you might just be saying that so I don't die of embarrassment."

"No, really." He rests his hands on my shoulders as if to reassure me, then slides his fingers down over my arms, rustling the tassels as he goes. "You look amazing. Like, really, really good."

His voice is soft and fervent, and his gaze never leaves my face. I feel another nervous quiver in the region of my stomach.

"Oh my God, that's *perfect*."

Cam releases me and steps back, and I have about two seconds to recover before Raven is in front of me with her half-eaten taco, beaming.

"Where the hell was Ms. Shelby hiding this?" She nudges Cam's arm with her elbow. "Did you find this? You're a *genius*. Well, what do you think, Jasper? Is it the one?"

I give myself one last chance to back out of the entire school seeing me in a sparkly rainbow pantsuit. But in the end, I can't deny it's a perfect outfit for the float, and I really do like how I look in it. "It's the one."

Raven claps her hands together. "Yes! I knew all we needed was to get some tacos in our system and everything would work out." She turns the full weight of a Vice President Raven stare onto me. "All right, take it off."

When I stare at her, she tugs my tasseled sleeve. "Take it off so I can go put it away with our other costumes. We don't want anybody else grabbing it before homecoming."

This time, I do salute. "Yes, ma'am."

Raven gives my shoulder a light smack, and I listen to her and Cam talking about unimportant stuff as I head back behind the folding screen to change. After I've peeled off the pantsuit, my fingers stray to where Cam's hand grazed over my arm, and then I pull on my sweatshirt and my jeans and join my friends.

Chapter Ten

I'm back on ticket duty with Felix, and day two is not off to an encouraging start. Felix nods at me as he slides into his chair but says nothing, and he buries himself in his phone before I can even attempt to make conversation. I'm just about to pull out my math notebook and get some homework done when he switches the phone off and tucks it into the pocket of his jeans.

"My girlfriend," he says with a vague gesture at his pocket. "She gets mad if I don't text her back right away."

I take a moment to absorb that he's actually making conversation with me.

"Even at school?"

He grimaces, which I take as a "yes."

"What happens if you don't answer?"

Another grimace. "It's not good."

I wonder if he even likes this girl, but for all that I'm hoping he might someday direct his romantic attentions in a more me-centric direction, I don't want to make any assumptions. Just because Felix is probably some manner of queer doesn't mean he's not interested in girls, or in this girl in particular.

"So how long have you been going out?" I ask.

"Since June. She asked me out on the last day of school." He hesitates, then adds, "She was in France with her family for the whole summer, so we didn't really see each other."

Ah.

"So really, you've only been going out for, like, a month."

"Yeah." There's silence for a beat, and then he glances in my direction without actually meeting my eyes. "Are you going out with that Rogers guy?"

I spend a second wondering who "Roger" is before I realize he's talking about Cam. "Oh. No, we're just friends."

"Hm," he says.

I hold the words in for as long as I can. "Why are you going out with someone you don't even like?"

Felix's gaze is wary. "Who says I don't like her?"

"I mean, do you?"

He folds his arms and shifts uncomfortably in his chair. "She's…fine."

"Huh," I say. "Okay."

"Anyway, who cares if I like her? She's *Hailey Oswald*, and she asked me out. Like I was gonna say no?"

"I mean, ideally, if you didn't like her, then…yeah?"

He scratches his fingernail against the tabletop. "You just don't get it."

"What don't I get?"

"When you're the captain of the varsity soccer team and a hot girl asks you out in front of everybody, you say yes."

"She asked you out in front of other people?"

More scratching. A groove is forming in the soft wood of the table. "Yeah. Ran up to me and kissed me in front of all the guys and asked me out." He tosses me a dark look. "Maybe it was some weird karmic payback for what I did to you."

The words stun me, and I'm not sure if I want to laugh or cry.

"Yeah," I say quietly, "but I wanted you to kiss me. Doesn't sound like you wanted it in this case."

I wait for him to deny it or snap at me, but all he does is sigh.

"Felix, you don't have to keep going out with her if you don't like her. And you don't have to stick with your friends if you don't like them. You don't have to live like this."

"You don't understand." His voice is barely a whisper. "This is who I am. This is all I have."

"That's not true. Seriously. You're so much more than this. And yeah, I know I haven't seen you in a long time, but if the Felix I knew is still in there, then you're way better than this, than all of them. Hell, you said it yourself. You're the captain of the varsity soccer team. You have a 4.0 average. In a few months, you're going to graduate and go off to some amazing college. You can do whatever you want, with whoever you want, and nobody can stop you. Nobody except you."

His eyes widen, and I glimpse a faint sheen of tears before he blinks it away. Then he jumps to his feet and runs off, and the squeaky door to the boys' bathroom opens and closes down the hall.

I sit. I breathe. I sip my soda and question my life choices.

When Felix hasn't come back ten minutes later, I grab the lockbox and creep down the hallway after him. The halls are empty since everyone is in class or at lunch, and the fluorescent light over my head flickers ominously like it thinks this is a horror movie.

When I take a tentative step into the bathroom, it seems empty. But the far stall door is closed, and faint, rapid breaths echo from that direction. I approach the stall and rest my hand on the door.

"Felix?" I keep my voice soft, questioning but not accusing. "Are you having an anxiety attack?"

"Go away." The words are low and strangled, and the harsh breathing continues.

"Would you open the door?"

He doesn't answer, but the bolt clicks, and the door creeps inward an inch. I push it open enough so I can slip into the stall.

Felix sits on the toilet lid with his legs drawn to his chest and his chin on his knees, eyes closed and sweat breaking out on his forehead. His hands tremble, and he's rocking back and forth a little. I hesitate, then step forward and press my hands gently to his shoulders. They're thin and shaking, and the urge to gather him in my arms and hug him until he feels better is hard to resist, even though I know that's not what he needs right now.

"Felix, look at me."

He squeezes his eyes shut more tightly, but finally they flutter open and stare up at me. They're liquid brown now, wet with tears and fear. I take a deep breath.

"You're fine, Felix. You're completely fine, and you can do this."

His eyes widen, and I know he remembers, too. Huddling together on his bedroom floor after a difficult dinner with his parents, his white-knuckled hand gripping mine as I asked him what I could do, how I could help. *Just tell me I'm fine.* His eyes were *squeezed shut, his voice shaky and fractured. "Tell me*

I'm fine, and that I can do this, and help me breathe."

His breath catches, and the frantic in and out of air slows a little, but he still throws me a desperate glance. "Help me breathe? Like you used to?"

I kneel in front of him, still cradling his shoulders. "Yeah, hey, of course. Look, focus on me. Focus on my breathing. Breathe in and out with me. Honestly, you're fine. You're absolutely fine. This is just a stupid panic attack, and you know how to get out of it. You can do it, I know you can."

We inhale and exhale together, and after a while, Felix's hands stop shaking, and his shoulders relax, and he sinks back against the wall of the stall and closes his eyes. His breathing is mostly back to normal now, slower and easier. My knees feel wobbly with relief as I rise to my feet.

"I always believe you," he croaks into the silence. "When you tell me I'm okay, I just believe you." He presses his hand over his eyes. "Jesus. I haven't had a panic attack in a really long time. Years, probably."

I wince. "Sorry."

"No, it's not your fault. Honestly, I think I just…" He drops his hand and glares at the floor. "I thought if I could be some other person, then maybe everything wouldn't be so hard. You know, if I could just be some straight dude-bro like Tyler, then nothing would be able to touch me. And it kinda worked, I guess. Nobody bullies me. I don't feel anxious most of the time. I just feel…numb. Empty. Like nothing matters."

I have no idea what to say to that, so I keep my mouth shut.

After a shaky exhale, Felix continues in a low voice. "I don't even know what I was expecting that day. It's not like I thought it through. If I'd been thinking at all, I wouldn't have done it on the freaking playground where other people could see us." His throat bobs as he swallows. "You know, I always wondered…"

"What?"

"I always wondered what would've happened if I'd kissed you somewhere else. Like, if we'd been in my room or out in that stupid fort we built in the woods or something. If I'd kissed you where no one could see us, would everything have been different? Would you have…" He looks up at me, his eyes large and dark and hopeful. "Would you have kissed me back?"

The question vibrates through my chest, flinging me back in time to a playground, a boy, an innocent collision of lips that changed everything. Felix holds my gaze, waiting, needing to hear me say the words.

"Felix…" I release a breath I've been holding since fifth grade. "Of course I would have."

The stall seems achingly small and intimate as he rises to his feet and takes a step toward me.

"Really?" he whispers.

My mouth is dry. I force a swallow, but my voice still comes out hoarse. "Really."

We stare at each other for a count of five, and I hardly breathe. Then Felix lifts his hand, hesitates, and rests it on my shoulder. The touch is warm, but I shiver anyway.

"Could I…" He takes another step, bringing us nose to nose. The scant space between our bodies vibrates with warmth and possibility. "Could we try it again?"

My voice is lost somewhere in the inch of space between us, so I just nod.

Felix leans in and presses his lips to mine.

It's barely a kiss, barely anything, but it means *everything*. Joy trembles through me, filling my veins with light, and my mind goes blissfully blank as I focus on the soft press of Felix's mouth, the way his fingers slide through my hair as he kisses me.

When our mouths separate, Felix leans our foreheads together, his breath tickling my lips and smelling like mint and the faint tang of tobacco. His eyes are large and vulnerable, and it hits me all over again that this is *Felix*. Felix is here in front of me, trusting me with this fragile, taped-together part of himself. A rush of protectiveness surges through me, and I wrap my arms around him.

He tenses at first, and I almost let go of him, but then something breaks and he clings to me, burying his face in my chest and squeezing his arms around me so tightly I stagger back a step. When I regain my balance, I just hold him and listen to his ragged breaths, content to live in this moment for as long as he needs.

"God, Jas." It's the first time he's said my name, and the sound of it in his soft, broken voice lodges in my chest and aches. "I don't know if I can do this. I don't think I even know how to be a good person anymore."

I rest my head against his. "You've always been a good person. Now you just have to let other people see it."

We cling to each other for a time longer, and then my foot bumps the lockbox with a screech of metal on bathroom tile.

Felix releases me and wipes a hand across his face, avoiding my eyes. "We should probably…"

"Get back," I say. "Yeah."

We don't speak as we slip out of the stall and back

into the world.

We spend the rest of our ticket-selling time talking quietly and occasionally throwing each other tentative smiles. Felix's fingers brush mine with increasing frequency, and our knees bump together under the table too often for it to be an accident. Once, Felix even rests his hand on my arm, and his smile grows with every second he leaves it there, like he's realizing the world won't end if he dares to touch a boy out where someone might see.

But I need to be realistic. One kiss and some light flirting isn't going to signal an instant change in Felix's life. It's not like he's going to immediately dump his friends and his girlfriend and join the QSA or something. But for the first time, I can see the old Felix in the face he shows me, and it's like coming home after a long, long time away.

Chapter Eleven

Cam shows up at the end of Lunch B just as Felix tosses me a shy wave and hurries off to his next class. Cam watches him go with a puzzled twist of a smile, then strides over to join me at the ticket table.

"So," he says. "I take it the Felix friendship initiative took some steps forward today?"

I sling my backpack over my shoulder and pick up the lockbox while Cam tosses my lunchtime garbage in the trash. "I guess you could say that."

We start down the hallway, and when I've done nothing but stare into the distance for a good fifteen seconds, Cam nudges my arm. "You don't have to tell me anything if you don't want to. But if you do want to talk about it…"

I debate with myself, then let out a breath. "There may have been a kiss. Of sorts."

Silence. When I risk a glance at Cam, his eyebrows are so high on his forehead they've vanished under his bangs.

I huff out an awkward laugh. "Yeah, I was surprised, too. And believe me, I did not expect our first kiss since fifth grade to happen in the boys' bathroom, but there you go."

A frown flits across Cam's face, but the next second he smiles and pats me on the back. "Well, hey, that's great! I mean, not the bathroom thing. That sounds a little unsanitary. But scoring a kiss on your second lunchtime together? He must really like you."

I chew on my lower lip. "I don't know, actually. He's just going through a lot. He's been going through a lot for a really long time, and I honestly don't know if anything is even going to come of this. But I mean, it was nice? I never thought he'd even want to talk to me again, let alone do something like that, so…yeah."

"I'm happy for you," Cam says. There's an odd note to his voice, but the warmth in his eyes is real.

Once we've dropped the lockbox and other homecoming stuff off in Mr. Harrison's room, Cam tucks his hands into his pants pockets and turns to me. "So are you seeing him again?"

"Felix? I mean, yeah, we still have to sell tickets…"

"I don't mean at school. If you really want the chance to see where this goes, you're probably going to want to spend time with him somewhere other than the boys' bathroom."

He has a point.

"Yeah. I guess I should, I don't know, ask him if he wants to hang out after school tomorrow?"

"There ya go."

"But you were gonna come over…"

Cam gives an easy shrug. "We can do that anytime. And if you guys end up getting together, you'll probably be spending a lot of time with him, anyway. I can't expect to keep you all to myself if you have a boyfriend, right?"

His tone is light, but there's a faint, fractured note underneath. My mind drifts to a few days earlier when I was at Cam's house, and his sister Alice ducked into the living room while Cam was putting in a load of laundry for their mom. At first, we talked about random stuff, most of it animal-related because it was Alice, but then she tilted her head to one side and studied me.

"You know, it's kinda funny."

"What is?" I asked.

"This. You guys. Cam's always been friendly with practically, like, everybody at school, but he's never been super close to anyone before. Usually he's just Mr. Big and Friendly Guy, the one everybody likes but nobody really knows, you know? And I know he's happy being that guy, but I think it gets kinda lonely sometimes." She gave a soft smile. "I'm glad he has you."

Warmth rippled through me, and I returned the smile. "I'm glad I have him, too."

I take hold of his arm, needing him to feel my reassurances as well as hear them. "Look, no matter what happens with Felix, I'm not going to forget about you, okay? You're my best friend. Probably the best friend I've ever had, and that's not going to change no matter how many boys I date."

He arches an amused eyebrow. "Exactly how many boys were you planning on dating?"

"You know what I mean. Seriously, Cam." I look straight into his eyes. "You and me? We're good. We're solid. Always, okay? No matter what."

He stares at me for another second, and then his arms wrap around me and pull me in. His hug envelops me, and I'm at just the right height to rest my head on his shoulder. When I held Felix, it was like holding a drowning man, like my arms were the only things keeping him from going under. But with Cam, it's just warmth and solidity and safety. Muscles I didn't realize

I was tensing relax, and I exhale a breath I didn't know I was holding.

When Cam releases me, he gives an awkward smile and scratches the back of his neck. "Er, sorry, was that too much?"

I laugh. "No. Hugs are good."

I lead the way to our next class, and we fall into easy conversation. I vow to myself that no matter what happens with Felix—or with any guy I might happen to have feelings for—I'll never turn my back on Cam. No matter what.

****

The QSA usually only meets on Fridays, but because it's homecoming this week and there's a ton to prepare, Raven and Cam have decided to hold after-school meetings every day this week. Today, there are around fifteen of us in the QSA room, some working on float decoration ideas while others chatter about the goods they'll be selling at the QSA booth at the fair this year. We're about ten minutes into the meeting when Jess appears in the doorway.

Raven goes still when she sees her, but Jess throws her a cheerful wave, and Raven mutters, "Be right back," to Cam before hurrying to the door. She and Jess slip out into the hallway together, out of sight and definitely out of eavesdropping range.

When I shift my attention back to the group, Lars Henry is watching me with a faint smile on their face. They're seated at the desk next to mine and have paused midway through a surprisingly skillful sketch of our parade float. "Finally," they say.

I glance over my shoulder like they might be talking to some invisible person behind me. "What?"

For all that we've been attending QSA meetings together since the first day of school, I haven't had much one-on-one interaction with Lars, though I've always thought they seemed pretty cool. Today, their chin-length white-blond hair is pulled back with a series of black clips, and a careful application of eyeliner makes their eyes look especially large and blue. They're wearing their usual T-shirt and skirt combo, though this time it's an artsy graphic tee of a starship soaring through light speed paired with a green tartan skirt.

Lars inclines their head toward the hallway. "Raven finally shooting her shot with Jess."

I glance back at the door where, of course, I can see nothing of Raven or Jess. "Is that what she's doing?"

"That's what she said." Their eyebrows shoot upward as they hurry on, "She told me she told you about it. I don't want you to think I'm the kind of person who goes around blabbing my best friend's romantic secrets to just anybody."

"I… No, yeah, of course. So you and Raven are best friends?"

Lars's thin shoulders lift in a shrug. "We've known each other since we were four years old. Next-door neighbors." They laugh, and it sounds a little strained. "Believe me, our parents started wondering if there was something in the water when we both ended up being some variety of trans."

"Are your…" I'm not sure I should even ask, but I've already started the question, so I spit the rest of it out. "Are your parents okay with it?"

Lars goes back to sketching, their pencil moving in smooth, easy strokes over the page. "Mine weren't really at first, but they got used to it. As for Raven, she just has her mom, but that lady worships her. The first thing she did after Raven came out was burst into tears and say she'd always wanted a daughter."

I've never met Raven's mom, but the image makes me smile. "That's awesome."

I'm just opening my mouth to ask another question when hurried footsteps pound closer, and a Raven-shaped blur sails past the door. She goes by too fast for me to get a good look at her face, but the choked breaths echoing down the hallway are unmistakable.

Lars and I exchange a grim look.

"Come on." They get to their feet. "I have a feeling this is a two-person job."

I'm not sure if I'm the right person for the task, but I still follow Lars out of the room and jog after them down the hall. We find Raven in the stairwell with her knees drawn to her chest and her face buried in her hands.

Lars drops down next to her and puts their arm around her, then motions for me to sit on the opposite side.

"You know I like Jess," Lars says in a low, dangerously calm voice, "but if she said anything transphobic to you, I will snap her drumsticks in half and throw them in the lake."

Raven gives a wavering laugh and rubs a hand across her eyes. Her fingers come away stained with mascara. "No, it's not that. I just… I couldn't do it. I was standing there in front of her, and she was looking up at me like she knew what I was going to say and might actually be into it, and the words wouldn't come. I chickened out."

Lars tightens their grip on her shoulders and sways

her back and forth. "Rave, that's nothing to be upset about. So you couldn't tell her today. There's always tomorrow."

"There aren't that many tomorrows left before we graduate, and every second I wait is another second she could get a girlfriend."

"But you said it seemed like she was into it," I venture. I'm still not entirely sure what I'm doing here, but I figure I should at least try to contribute. "If she does like you, I doubt she's going to go get a girlfriend just like that."

"Unless I was just imagining it." Raven sighs deeply. "I think that's what really stopped me from saying something. Because if I go into this thinking I have no chance with her, then it's fine if she turns me down. I mean, not fine, but it's not *devastating*. But if I actually think she might like me, and she doesn't…"

The pain is thick in her voice, and it actually hurts me to hear it.

"Either way, it's better to know, isn't it?" Lars asks softly. "And we've gotten through 'devastated' before. We can do it again."

"I don't exactly want to do it again."

"It's either that or more of this. Risk devastation, or exist in a miserable half-life for the rest of the year. Your choice, babe."

Raven shoots them a dry look. "You're really not great at this comforting thing, you know."

Lars smiles and brushes a lock of Raven's hair out of her eyes. "Just trying to be realistic. Anyway, I'm here as the voice of reason. Jasper's here to be the comfort guy."

Both of them turn to look at me.

"Um… There, there?"

Raven laughs, and I don't feel like such a complete failure at being a supportive friend. With Lars's arm still around her shoulders, she wipes the last of the wetness from her cheeks and climbs to her feet.

"Come on." She lifts her chin and gives a brave sniff. "I've got a meeting to run, and you two need to get back to work."

By the time we get back to the QSA room, Raven is back to her usual self, confident and in control, effortlessly solving problems and sorting out every issue that's brought to her. But Lars watches her carefully as the meeting goes on, and more than once the two of us lock eyes and exchange a sad sort of grimace. I'm not sure how to help Raven, but it definitely makes me feel better to know she has someone like Lars on her side.

And even though I'm not anywhere near as handy in a crisis, she's got me, too.

Chapter Twelve

I'm not sure what to expect the next day at the ticket booth. Has Felix been thinking about yesterday as much as I have? Or has he already convinced himself it was a mistake and gone back to being the homophobic dude-bro Felix of my nightmares?

When he turns the corner and spots me sitting there, his eyes light up, and relief trembles through me. He's grinning by the time he sits down beside me, and even though people are milling around the hallway not too far from us, he takes my hand under the table and squeezes it.

"Hey," he says.

I blink down at the warm tangle of our fingers and try to remember how to speak.

"Hey."

"So I kind of have some news." He's still holding my hand, a fact my brain reminds me of approximately every point-two seconds.

"Okay…"

"I dumped Hailey."

My heart jolts in my chest. "Seriously?"

"Yeah. Yesterday after school. I told her I don't feel that way about her, and we broke up."

"Huh." I don't want to make too big a deal out of this in case it doesn't mean what I think it means, but inside, I'm freaking out. "Well. How are you feeling about all that?"

The grin pulls at his lips again, and he looks so much like the ten-year-old Felix in my memory I kind of want to cry. Or maybe just hug him and never let go. "Really good, actually. You were right yesterday. I never liked her, not like that and…not at all, really. She's kind of mean, and I don't think we ever had a conversation that wasn't her either complaining about her parents not buying her something or making fun of somebody. So yeah, I'm pretty glad I don't have to listen to that anymore."

"That's awesome." I squeeze his hand. "I'm really proud of you."

He beams at me, and I'm struck all over again by how a simple smile can transform him from a moody stranger into the boy I knew when we were ten.

I clear my throat and attempt a casual tone. "So if you're not Hailey's boyfriend anymore, I'm guessing that means you'll have a little bit more free time. Like, after school, for example. Maybe to hang out with someone else, if you wanted to?"

Felix's smile is dry. "Were you this awkward when we were kids?"

"Probably way more, actually. But yeah, would you maybe want to hang out after school today? It doesn't have to be anywhere public. You're welcome to come back to my house if you want, or…whatever."

I expect him to need a minute to think about it, but he immediately holds out his hand. "Yeah, absolutely. Give me your phone."

When I peer over his shoulder, he's inputting a new contact named "Felix."

"Text me your address," he says. "I have soccer

practice, but I can come by after. Maybe a little after six, if that's not too late?"

"Yeah, you can even stay for dinner if you want. Dad's gotten used to making enough food for an army since Cam's always over at our house, so I'm sure he won't mind."

Felix's smile stiffens, just for a second, and he gives my hand one last warm squeeze before letting go.

****

Our ticket-selling time goes well for the most part, particularly since we have a grand total of four customers and otherwise just smile sappily at each other and talk. Felix gives me a run-down of how he got into soccer (his dad thought it would be good for him to have an extracurricular that might get him out of his shell, and Felix ended up loving it and actually having a natural talent for it), and I tell him about my two misguided years of thinking I could play the trombone before I realized I really, really couldn't.

We're laughing about Dad wearing earplugs around the house to block out my trombone torture sessions when a flicker of movement catches my eye. I turn to find one of the last people I want to see sauntering up to us.

"Yo, Morales!"

I shift the remaining half of my sandwich closer to me and carefully set my can of orange soda on the floor at my feet.

"Hey." Felix sounds wary, and while I'm glad to see he hasn't shifted his chair away from mine, there's a new tension in his shoulders. "You skipping again?"

Tyler shrugs. "Just wasn't feeling it today. Anyway, that Fenton kid's my lab partner, so I'll get a good grade whether I'm there or not. Nothing like having a big ole nerd doing all the work, am I right?"

Felix gives a weak chuckle but doesn't reply.

Tyler hasn't even glanced in my direction. Guess I still don't exist.

"Hey so there's something I want to talk to you about." He lowers his voice as he leans over our table. "Hailey's really upset, man. She was crying, like, all morning, and I know you've probably got a plan in mind, but don't string her along for too long, okay?"

Felix frowns. "What do you mean?"

"I mean, it's a great strategy, dude. Dump her, let her cry for a bit, then pick her back up again and she'll do anything you want, right? It's a solid strat, but I'm telling you, I know Hailey, and it's not going to take her long to go from missing you to hating your freaking guts. Just make sure you jump back in there before she gets to the hating you part, okay?"

I want to throw up. Or give Tyler's empty head a shake and see if anything falls out but dust and misogyny.

Instead, I wait to see what Felix will say. He's spent years suppressing everything he is to fit in with these guys, and a few days with me isn't going to undo all of that.

To my surprise, he lifts his chin. "Actually, I don't want to get back together with her. I broke up with her because I like somebody else."

I look sharply at Felix. His face is calm, but his hands are shaking in his lap. It takes all my restraint not to grab hold of them.

Tyler regards Felix with what I guess is the soccer god version of respect. "No way, man, you got somebody else? Hotter than Hailey?"

Felix's lips twitch. "I mean, yeah, I think so."

I swallow a semi-hysterical laugh. *Oh my God.*

Tyler lands a few solid bro-punches on Felix's shoulder. The guy is practically bouncing with excitement. "Dang, dude, that's awesome. So when do I get to meet the new mystery girl?"

My breath catches, and I fight to keep a neutral expression so I won't give away whatever lie Felix is about to spin.

But Felix looks Tyler straight in the eye and says, "It's not a girl, man. I'm gay."

Chapter Thirteen

Tyler laughs. It's a harsh sound, echoing off the metal lockers. "Good one, dude. But seriously, who's the girl?"

"I am being serious. There's no girl, Tyler. I'm gay."

An unsteady chuckle works its way from Tyler's throat, and he falls back a step. "Um, no you're not."

Felix offers a faint half smile. "Pretty sure I am."

For the first time, Tyler's eyes flicker over to me. "What, you spend a few lunchtimes with this homo, and suddenly you're gay?"

I expect Felix to flinch under the pressure of dude-bro homophobia, but he sits taller in his chair and levels a calm, deadly stare on Tyler. "No, I've always been gay. You gonna call me names, too?"

Tyler is the one who flinches this time, wilting under the icy, unblinking stare of his captain. His hands clench and unclench at his sides, and I wait for the yelling to start, but he just mutters, "Whatever, man," and stalks off down the hallway.

When he's gone, Felix exhales a shaky breath and sinks into his chair like a deflated balloon.

"I can't believe you did that," I say.

He presses a trembling hand over his eyes. "I can't believe I did that, either. But I just... I don't want to go back to that, you know? I don't want to be like those guys anymore. And I knew if I didn't say it right then, I might never say it."

His fingers are still shaking, so I take them in mine and squeeze.

"God, Felix. Are you all right? I mean, seriously, are you okay?"

"I think I actually am. Tyler's a prick, but I'm his captain. I can get him kicked off the team if he's a piece of crap about this, and he knows it. I'm not saying it's all going to be fine, but it felt so freaking good to finally say that to him. Am I in shock? I might be in shock."

I bring our clasped hands to my chest. "What you are," I say, "is a freaking badass."

His eyes are bright as they fix on mine. "If I am, it's because of you. You told me I could do this, Jas. You really believed I could, and you know what? You were right. I lost myself for a while, like, really and truly lost who I was, but I'm done doing that now. I'm done being that guy. I want to be Felix again, the real one." He leans close to me, so close our noses are nearly touching, and my heartbeat stutters as a soft exhalation of breath whispers against my cheek. "The one who wasn't afraid to kiss you in front of everybody."

And then he does it. He kisses me. In the school hallway, across from the windowed doors of the lunchroom, where anyone could glance out and see us. His fingers graze my cheek, and his kiss is gentle and seeking, a question and a promise.

When we pull apart, we're both smiling.

No one jeers, no one laughs. Probably no one even saw. I press my forehead to his and run my fingers along his jaw. It's rough with a dusting of stubble, and I like the prickly feel of it under my hand.

"I missed you so much," he whispers. "You don't

even know."

I shake my head. "I think I might have an idea."

When we pull apart and settle back into our chairs, Felix reaches across the table for a pen that's rolled dangerously near the edge. As he does so, his sleeve shifts back, and I catch a flash of beige on his upper arm.

"What's that?"

He follows my gaze and quickly tugs the sleeve back down. "Oh, um. It's nothing."

"No, seriously, what is it? Did you get hurt or something?"

"No, I just…" He sighs. "It's a nicotine patch, okay?"

I burst out laughing.

Felix folds his arms, his lips pursing into a pout that morphs into a grin. "Go ahead and laugh, but a wise sage once told me I'll 'croak' if I keep smoking, and I figured it was time to listen to him."

"Hey, I was just quoting. But I'm glad you're doing it. Lung cancer's no joke, and I want you to be around for a long time."

Felix stares at me, and I wonder if I've said too much. It's not like I'm proposing or anything, it's just now that he's back in my life, I don't want to think of a future without him in it.

"Thanks," he says softly. "And not just for saying that. For everything."

I smile, and he smiles back. And for the first time since fifth grade, I know we're going to be all right.

****

The rumors start that afternoon. Cam and I are in our customary seats at the back of the Economics room, waiting for class to start, when Ashley López drops into her seat in front of me and spins to face her best friend Keiko.

"Oh my God, did you hear?"

"What?"

"You know Felix Morales?"

"Um, yeah, duh."

"Well, turns out he's *gay*. Can you believe it?"

Keiko shoots her a dry look. "Are you sure that's not just some rumor Hailey's spreading around? He did just dump her, and you know how she is."

"No, and that's the craziest part. Apparently he told Tyler Bruce the reason he dumped Hailey is, get this, because he's in love with some guy."

"Well dang. What guy?"

"Nobody knows, but maybe it's somebody else on the soccer team? I mean, you spend enough time with a bunch of buff, half-naked guys and something's bound to happen, right?"

Keiko rolls her eyes. "That's not how being gay works, moron."

"Well, whatever. All I know is this is *huge*. I mean, do you think Felix will still get to be captain of the soccer team?"

"Why wouldn't he?"

"I don't know, guys are weird about stuff like this. Maybe they won't feel comfortable having him on the team anymore."

"Well, that'd be pretty dumb. He's the best player they have. No way they'd have a shot at State without him."

"I'm just saying. Guys are weird sometimes."

"*You're* weird."

"Shut up."

They switch topics to what they're doing this weekend, but I stop listening. My mouth is dry, my stomach twisting. Even Cam's jaw is tight, his expression grim.

Felix being open with Tyler is one thing, but having the whole school know? Ashley's right. Guys *are* weird about stuff like this. How long will it be until some soccer bro starts feeling uncomfortable about Felix being in the changing room with them, or wonders if maybe a guy who likes guys shouldn't be captaining a boys' sports team? It's ridiculous, but some people really do feel that way.

I groan and close my eyes. Cam's warm hand presses into my arm, and I take what comfort I can from the touch.

****

After school, Cam finds me skulking by the soccer field, not far from where the marching band is practicing. He doesn't say anything, just hands me a French vanilla cappuccino from the coffee shop down the road and settles beside me on the grass. We press our backs to the metal edge of the bleachers and sip our drinks.

"Is Raven mad I'm not at the meeting?" The coffee is perfect, rich and creamy and exactly as sweet as I like it.

He shrugs. "I told her something important came up. Her eye only twitched a little, so I think we're fine." He glances beyond my shoulder. "So we're spying on the soccer team, then?"

The aforementioned team are toy-sized figures at the opposite end of the field, dashing back and forth in some mysterious sporty training activity.

"Yeah, I just… I'm worried. I know he's the captain

and everything, but what if they start treating him like crap now?"

"Do you think you'll be able to tell how they're treating him from all the way over here?"

"Probably not, but I just feel better being here. Maybe I won't even see it, and maybe there's nothing I can do, but I don't want him to be alone."

Cam's expression softens. "I get it."

We sit close enough for our shoulders to touch, and I enjoy his warm, solid presence beside me as I drink my coffee. It's the kind of fall day my dad likes to call "crisp," and the sky is impossibly blue above us, only obscured by a few faint white wisps of clouds. The sunlight has turned to late afternoon gold, and the distant, cheery shouts from the soccer team blend with the musical cacophony of the marching band playing what is either "When the Saints Go Marching In" or "Bad Romance" by Lady Gaga.

"You know," Cam says after a while, "we could go closer if you wanted."

My tense muscles were starting to unknot, but anxiety surges through me again. "Things are probably rough enough for Felix right now without me waltzing up to his soccer practice like a flashing gay neon sign."

Cam snorts into his cocoa. "We wouldn't have to go sit in the middle of the field or anything. There's already a bunch of people sitting up in the bleachers. We could infiltrate."

"Infiltrate?"

"Yeah, we'll pretend we're soccer groupies and try to blend in. Quick, name a soccer move."

"Um…kicking?"

"I'll allow it." He fixes me with one of his too-perceptive stares. "Look, you're not doing any good hiding out over here where you can't even see what's going on. And who knows, maybe Felix will be glad to know you came to support him. This has gotta be scary for him, being out to his teammates. If I were him, I'd want to know my boyfriend had my back."

The word "boyfriend" fizzes in my brain and causes a small neural avalanche. "I... He's not my boyfriend."

"Whatever he is, he clearly likes you. And you came here because you're worried about him. So let's go make sure he's okay and show him he's not alone out there."

I get to my feet. My heart is beating like crazy, but I force my voice to be steady. "Okay. Let's infiltrate."

We creep along the edge of the bleachers until we reach the section closest to where the soccer team is practicing. Just as Cam said, scattered groups of students sit here and there, and it's easy enough for us to slip among them and find seats about three-fourths of the way up the bleachers. No one even glances at us as we settle in, and I have to admit it's nice to actually see what's going on.

I scan the mass of uniformed bodies on the field and quickly find Felix. He's standing on the edge of the field with an older guy in a baseball cap who I assume is the coach.

I watch, mesmerized by the easy confidence I never saw in Felix when we were kids. He shouts orders at the team, and they snap to follow. He exchanges words with the coach, then strolls up and down the field, studying the exercises the rest of the team are doing. At one point, he shows a skinny red-haired kid a better way to kick the ball, and the kid beams like it's made his whole life.

After a while, the team breaks into two groups for a

practice game, and Felix becomes a blur of green streaking down the field, effortlessly juggling the ball between his feet before slamming it into the opposite goal. He's swarmed by his nearby teammates, who laugh and cheer as they slap him on the back.

They're about midway through the match when I turn to Cam. He's been silent up to now, watching and sipping his drink.

"It's like they don't even care," I say. "I mean, they must know. They *have* to know. It's all over school. But they're not treating him any differently. They're acting like he's still their captain, like they still like him and, you know, respect him."

Cam's eyebrow twitches. "Are you disappointed?"

"No! Just…surprised."

And I really freaking am. The only hint of anything wrong I see out there is Tyler, who keeps frowning over at Felix and missing the ball when it gets passed to him, but he doesn't look angry or grossed out so much as confused. Mac zips around the field like a lightning bolt, giving Felix some much-needed competition, but he still laughs and exchanges friendly taunts with Felix when they pass each other. And Muncher, who is surprisingly agile as the goalie for Felix's team, yells and cheers along with the rest of them every time Felix scores.

When the practice game is over, with Felix's side winning 5-2, the coach gathers the team, and they form a huddle with heads in the center and arms around each other. Mac is on one side of Felix, and some random guy is on the other, and neither of them hesitate before sliding their arms around his shoulders. Felix's voice rises in encouraging words I can make out the tone of but not the content, and then the whole team docs some kind of chant that ends in a cheer with their fists upraised.

And that's it. Soccer practice is over, and Felix is fine.

I get to my feet, thinking Cam and I can slip away before Felix notices us, but the movement must catch Felix's eye because suddenly he's staring right at me. I freeze, but a grin breaks out on his face, and he jogs toward us. Cam gives my shoulder a nudge, and I take a deep breath and make my way down the bleachers.

Felix is flushed and beaming, and there's a little smudge of dirt on his cheek I barely stop myself from wiping away.

"Hey," I say.

"Hey." His gaze flickers past my shoulder, I assume at Cam still sitting in the bleachers. "Were you here the whole time?"

"Um, most of it." I feel oddly bashful standing here with Felix in front of so many people, but I know that's silly. "I just wanted to make sure you were, you know. That you were okay."

A pleased smile tugs at his lips. "Yeah?"

"Yeah. I was worried about you. But I'm glad... I mean, it looks like everything is okay?"

Felix glances over his shoulder at the team, most of whom are picking up cones from the field or packing up other equipment. "Yeah, I guess it kind of is. I'm sure everybody knows. Tyler told Hailey, and of course Hailey told *everyone*. But no one's given me any crap for it so far. Even in the locker room, everybody was just...normal. Like nothing's changed."

This should make me happy. It's what Felix deserves, what all queer kids deserve, to have news like this be treated like it's no big deal. But I can't help wondering if Felix was just some random senior—not the varsity soccer captain, not top of the class, not a good-looking popular guy—would everyone be reacting this well to him coming out?

"That's great," I manage.

To my surprise, Felix takes my hand and swings it between us while peering shyly at my face. "You still okay with me coming over tonight?"

A swarm of butterflies takes up residence in my stomach. "Um, yeah, if you still want to."

"Yeah, just let me go get changed and shower and stuff. Do you want me to meet you there, or are you going to hang around?"

"I can wait for you."

He squeezes my hand and jogs back over to the team, leaving me staring after him feeling the ground shifting under my feet. I think back to Sunday, Felix leaning against the church wall smoking and scowling at me, and I honestly can't believe just a few days have changed things so drastically.

Someone comes up behind me, and I turn, thinking it's Cam, but it's Jess. Her red curls are tucked under a knit cap, and her hands are stuffed into the pockets of a puffy green and white marching band jacket. The band seems to be on a break, people wandering around, sitting in the grass, or blowing vaguely rude sounds on trumpets and trombones.

"Hey," she says. Her gaze flickers from me to Felix's retreating form, and she smiles a little but doesn't comment. "So you're friends with Raven, right?"

"Uh, yeah. We're friends."

Up close, I see that Jess has a small, upturned nose with a smattering of freckles across it, and there's a tiny silver stud in her left nostril. She's almost a head shorter than me, and that plus her soft, curvy frame makes her look, to quote Raven, "unbearably cute and huggable." Seriously, that girl has it bad.

"Look…" Jess kicks at a stone on the grass and avoids my eyes. "Maybe I shouldn't be asking you this, but is she okay? She's been acting really weird lately, and I'm starting to get kind of worried about her. I just wanted to make sure nothing happened. Like, nobody died, she didn't just get diagnosed with a terminal disease, or lose her dog or something…"

I swallow a startled laugh. "As far as I know, it's nothing like that."

"Okay, phew. Well, that's good, at least." Her green eyes focus on my face, and I resist the urge to fidget. "So then, I guess whatever's bothering her has to do with…something else? Something to do with me, maybe?"

My mouth falls open. "Sorry, I really don't think it's my place to—"

"No, no, you're totally right, forget about it." Jess gives a hurried wave of her hand, her eyes widening. "Sorry, I shouldn't have asked. I don't want to make you betray her trust or anything. Just tell her I asked about her, okay? And whatever she wanted to tell me yesterday, if she wants to try telling me again? I'm around. That's all, I guess."

She heads back to band practice, and I'm still staring after her when a warm shoulder bumps gently against mine.

"Hey," Cam says. "You okay?"

I genuinely have no idea, but I also don't know how to explain the tangle of emotions going on inside me right now. "Yeah, I'm good."

Cam sends a wincing glance toward the stands. "That's good, because I think your secret might be out."

My stomach drops as I turn. A group of girls watches me from the bleachers, most of them grinning knowingly and at least one waggling her eyebrows.

"Oh no."

Cam grimaces. "Yeah, I guess Felix walking up to you with hearts in his eyes and then holding your hand was a little bit of a clue. Looks like they may have figured out you're his mystery man."

I groan, but it was bound to happen eventually, wasn't it? And this particular group doesn't look disapproving. They look weirdly excited, like me dating Felix is some thrilling new development in their favorite teen drama.

Cam peers at me. "You need me to run interference? I can go treat them to some of polka's greatest hits while you make a run for it, if you want."

I snort, and some of the tension drains out of me. "Much as I want to see that, I think I'm good. I mean, this is the best-case scenario, right? People knowing and being okay with it?"

Cam's gaze lingers on my face a moment too long before he rocks back on his heels and tucks his hands into his jacket pockets. "Well, in that case, I should probably head home. Mom wants me to make dinner, and I'm thinking I might wow her with my homemade lasagna for some best-son-ever brownie points."

I raise my eyebrows. "Lasagna, huh? Last time I came over, we had frozen dinners."

"Hey, frozen dinners are quick, which means I can spend more time with you. I figured it'd be kind of rude to leave you alone for two hours while I whipped up something more gourmet."

"I could've helped."

He shoots me a fond look. "Don't take this the wrong way, Jasper, but I've seen what you can do in the kitchen. And your dad has told me stories. Horrible, terrifying stories."

"Hey, I may have set the stove on fire *once*, but I was eleven and poorly supervised. I've learned a lot since then."

"Even so, I think it's probably safer if I'm the cook in this relationship." His eyes widen. "This friendship, I mean. Anyway, I better get going. Have fun with Felix."

He gives my shoulder one last friendly pat and heads off, and I'm not prepared for the tug in my gut that makes me want to follow him.

Chapter Fourteen

With Cam gone, I settle in at the edge of the bleachers and pull out my phone. The soccer team has retreated into the locker rooms to get cleaned up and changed, and most of the groupies have left, even the Felix/Jasper fangirls. Only a few people are still hanging around the bleachers, but none of them seem interested in me, and that suits me just fine.

While I wait, I tap out a text to Raven, letting her know what happened with Jess. I get a notification that she read the message and three little "typing" dots pop up, but then they vanish and never reappear. Before I can decide if I should text her again to ask if she's okay, I hear the rhythm of running feet and look up to see Felix jogging toward me.

He's all long legs and smooth strides, his wavy brown hair streaming behind him. Even back in the jeans and green hoodie he wore to school today, he looks every inch the popular soccer star. I get to my feet as he approaches, but instead of slowing to a stop, he crashes into me and spins me around.

I burst out laughing, more out of surprise than anything else, and wrap my arms around him to keep from falling over.

"What the hell, Felix?"

He laughs and averts his eyes as he catches his breath. "Sorry, I'm just... I'm happy, I guess."

The words melt something inside of me. "Yeah?"

He gives a shy smile as he loops his arm in mine. "Yeah."

We head to the parking lot and track down the clunker, which doesn't take long since it's the oldest, crappiest car in the lot. Felix takes in the chipping pale-green paint, the dent in the fender, and the boxy shape that went out of style at least ten years before either of us were born.

"Nice ride." There's only a suggestion of sarcasm in his voice. "Your uncle Ronnie?"

I nod as I slide into the driver's seat. "Who knew it'd be so handy to have an uncle who owns a junkyard?"

Felix shakes his head as he fastens his seat belt. "Super handy if you want to drive a piece of junk."

"Hey!" I bring a hand to my heart as if he's deeply wounded me. "Be nice to my boy. He may not be much to look at, but he's got it where it counts."

"Aren't cars usually 'she'?"

"Yeah, for some reason the whole female car thing just never appealed to me. No idea why."

Felix laughs. "It's a mystery."

We pull out of the lot, and while it feels good to have Felix sitting beside me, I also have no idea what to say to him. I feel flushed and nervous, and I keep starting to say something and then stopping myself because I think it'll sound dumb. Felix doesn't speak either, staring at the passing scenery with his hair dancing around in the breeze from the open window, and I tell myself this will get easier. It's bound to be a little awkward at first, but once we get used to being around each other again, we'll fall back into our old rhythms and be completely fine.

In desperation, I flick on the radio, and Felix and I

both wince as accordion music blares from the speakers.

"Oh my God, what *is* that?" He presses his hands over his ears as I fumble to turn down the volume.

"That," I say, "is polka."

"Are my ears bleeding? I feel like my ears are bleeding."

"No ear-related blood that I can see. I think you're fine."

"I'll be a lot more fine once you change the station. Did your dad leave that on or something?"

I twist the knob a few times and land us on a classic rock station. It's a thousand times better, but I still feel the need to say, "I mean, it's not *that* bad. When you get used to it, it's kind of fun."

Felix shakes his head. "I feel like we might have very different ideas about what 'fun' means."

We go the rest of the short ride without speaking, nodding our heads to music led by guitars instead of accordions, and all too soon we pull into my driveway.

The house is quiet as I lead the way inside, and my pulse thrums in my throat with nerves and a quiet thrill of anticipation. Dad is running a D&D campaign at the game store tonight, a fact that slipped my mind when I invited Felix over.

"Dad doesn't get home 'til late on Wednesday, so he lets Cam and me order in pizza," I say as I drop my bookbag on the kitchen island. "Are you hungry? We can order it right away or wait a while, whatever you want to do."

Felix hovers in the kitchen doorway with his arms crossed, looking as awkward as I feel. "Um, yeah, sure, whatever you want to do."

I laugh. "We can't both say 'whatever you want to

do.' One of us has to make a decision."

"Sorry." He takes a step forward, then stops. "I guess I'm just a little…"

"Nervous?"

He nods. "Is that dumb?"

"If it is, then I'm dumb, too."

"Maybe we could talk for a little while first? Before we get dinner, I mean."

"Yeah sure." I lead Felix into the living room and drop onto the tan cushions of the couch. He hesitates and then sits beside me, close but not close enough that our shoulders touch.

I stare at the vase of flowers next to the TV. Felix looks down at his hands. I wonder if either of us will ever speak again.

"Look," I say, "why don't we start with something easy? How was your day today?"

"It was fine. Good." A smile teases at his lips. "Some parts were very good."

I echo the smile. "Oh, yeah? Like what?"

"Like kissing you in the hallway. And you coming to soccer practice. And the whole soccer team not freaking out when they found out I'm gay."

"So you think you're gay, then?" When Felix arches an eyebrow, I rush to add, "I mean, you're not bi or pan or something else."

"No, I'm pretty sure I'm gay. I've never been interested in a girl, not ever."

I chew on my lower lip. "What about boys?"

"I mean, there was you. Back in fifth grade, I definitely had a thing for you, though I didn't realize it until later. Wanting to kiss you probably should've clued me in, but what can I say? I was a dumb kid."

"If you were dumb, I don't want to think about what I was."

He breathes a soft laugh. "I definitely had a huge crush on you back then, and after that... I didn't really let myself feel anything for other guys. I always noticed them, though. It's hard not to when you play sports. There were one or two guys I probably could've had crushes on if I'd let myself, but I never did. I just pushed it all down and tried to ignore it."

"Doesn't sound very healthy," I say.

"Handling things in a healthy way isn't really how I operate. I'm a lot better at repressing stuff and being an absolute prick for years at a time."

I prop my elbow on the back of the couch and lean my head against my palm. "I don't think you were an absolute prick."

"How would you know?"

"I watched you at soccer practice today, dude. Those guys love you. That kid you were helping with his kicks looked like he worshipped you. You might not have been a saint all the time, but you didn't do as good a job of burying nice Felix as you thought."

He mirrors my posture, and a tingle goes through me as his warm brown eyes gaze into mine. "I haven't been happy in a really long time," he says softly. "There were things here and there that didn't suck, like winning a game or hanging out with the guys. But I wasn't happy. Not like I was back when we were friends."

The all-too-familiar guilt gnaws at me. "I'm sorry."

"You don't have to apologize."

"I do. I owe you a whole freaking lifetime of apologies."

"Well, then, what about me? You did one bad thing

117

when you were ten years old. I've been a jerk for years." His gaze drops, and so does his voice. "I bullied people, Jas. I bullied—"

"Cam," I say, and Felix's eyes snap up to meet mine. "He told me."

There's a long silence. "What did he say?"

"Just that your friends used to bully him when he was younger, and you were there, too."

"Did he tell you I outed him?"

I blink. "What?"

Felix's jaw is tight, his eyes downcast. "He came out to me, and I turned around and told the guys, and they used it to bully him for a whole freaking year. I did that."

The air rushes out of my lungs, and I stare at Felix as I wait for the oxygen to return.

"When I first started school here," he says, "Cameron and I were in Choir together. It was just one class, but he was the first person who actually tried to be my friend. I wasn't playing soccer yet, so I was just the weird new kid who didn't say much. But he started talking to me, and he was nice and funny, and I just... I liked him. When I told him my dad wanted me to try out for soccer, he was really encouraging about it. I was super nervous, but he gave me this pep talk before tryouts, and it really helped.

"Anyway, I got on the team, and when people realized I was a pretty good player, they started wanting to be my friend. Tyler was the first one, and then Mac and Muncher and some of the other guys, and pretty soon we were winning games, and people at school actually knew who I was, and they liked me. I still talked to Cameron in Choir, but he was this chubby kid who was always wearing T-shirts with princesses on them, and

Tyler and the guys thought that was hilarious. They thought I was talking to him as a joke or something.

"I wanted them to stop laughing at him, so I told Cameron he should stop wearing stuff like that. I told him the soccer guys thought he was gay because of all the princess stuff, and he said, 'Well, I kind of am.' We were literally in the middle of the hallway and anybody could've heard him, but he goes, 'Yeah, I like boys and girls both.' Like it didn't matter. Like he wasn't ashamed at all. He was just happy and comfortable being who he was, and it made me so *angry*."

"So you told Tyler and the other guys."

"And I didn't feel bad about it, either. Cameron was nothing but nice to me that whole time, and I let my friends make his life miserable. Just because I was jealous. So honestly, don't apologize to me. Don't ever apologize. I'm the last person who deserves an apology."

Silence falls between us, and I sit in it for a while. I want to be angry at Felix, furious he put Cam through all that, but all I feel is sad. Sad for Cam, sad for Felix, sad that queer kids still have to go through this crap just to be who they are.

"Have you ever apologized to him?" I ask.

He shakes his head. "I don't think that'd do any good."

"You might be surprised. Cam's not holding a grudge against you, Felix. He's been helping me this whole time. Hell, he's the one who took me to your church and got us working together selling homecoming tickets. He's the whole reason we're even sitting here right now. So if you apologize to him, I'm pretty sure he'll be okay with it."

Felix falls back against the couch cushions and

breathes a weak laugh. "Seriously, what is with that guy? How can anybody be that nice?"

I laugh, too. "It's just how he is. He's like if sunshine was a person. Sometimes I feel like I could literally tell him I just murdered somebody, and he'd be like, 'That's okay, I'm sure you had a good reason.' "

Felix smiles but doesn't look at me when he speaks. "You really like him, huh?"

"Well, yeah, of course. And I'm sure you'll really like him, too, once you spend some time with him again. Maybe we could all hang out together sometime?"

There's a pause. "Yeah," he says. "Maybe."

Chapter Fifteen

We order the pizza, half smothered in toppings for me, half plain cheese for Felix, and turn on the TV while we wait. It's still set to the teen drama network Cam and I started watching ironically and are now completely addicted to.

"I thought this was a murder mystery or something." Felix's eyes are wide as we stare at the beautiful twenty-five-year-old teens on the screen.

"That was only season one," I say. "After that, it got a little…"

"Wait, are those babies *floating?*"

"A little weird," I conclude. "But at least we get to see A.A. on a pretty frequent basis."

Felix arches an eyebrow. "Alcoholics Anonymous?"

"Archie's Abs. They're kind of a character all on their own, so Cam and I figured they needed a name. It's also kind of funny because Archie's actor goes by K.J., and so we have this joke that K.J. and A.A. are brothers, but K.J. is jealous because A.A. gets all the attention, but…"

I trail off as Felix frowns at me, an unmistakable suggestion of "what the hell" in the furrow of his brow.

"Never mind."

We settle into silence, and Felix slides his arm around my shoulders. It's cozy and warm and nice, but my head is used to leaning against a different shoulder, broad and solid where Felix is bony and lean. When Felix laughs, it's a lower sound than I'm expecting and never synchs up with mine, and the room feels emptier, too, like Felix and I don't quite fill up the space on our own.

But I don't want to think about that, so I focus on Felix's face.

It really is unbelievable how much he's changed. I always liked the way he looked, but nowadays he's objectively beautiful, all smooth brown skin and cheekbones and full lips. My gaze keeps tracking back to his mouth, and I feel like I should kiss him—I should want to kiss him right now—but I'm content to just sit with my arm around him, watching his face and feeling the warmth of his body seeping into mine.

Eventually, he catches me looking at him and throws me a quizzical frown, but it melts quickly as he slides his fingers along my jaw and lifts my chin.

His lips press to mine, and it's warm and soft, everything it was last time and the time before. And I like it, I do, but I pull back before it can deepen into anything more. I settle for linking our fingers and resting our clasped hands on my leg, squeezing Felix's hand so he knows he's done nothing wrong. I feel his gaze on my face, but then he shrugs and nestles back against me, his head falling into place on my shoulder.

****

Some time later, we sit shoulder to shoulder on the living room carpet with our backs to the couch, eating pizza while we play a game we call "Do You Still."

It's Felix's turn, and I enjoy the look of concentration on his face as he thinks. Brow knitted, gaze directed upward and to the left, lips pressed in a thin line.

"Okay, I've got one," he says. "Do you still hate oatmeal raisin cookies?"

I nod solemnly. "They are an abomination and have no business looking like chocolate chip cookies when they're not. Do you still like those weird space movies with Duke Skyhopper or whatever his name is?"

His mouth hangs open for a solid three seconds before it snaps shut again. "I know you're joking, but it still hurts me, Jasper. Show some respect for the best science fiction franchise of all time."

"I mean, technically it's more of a space fantasy than science fiction…"

"I'm not having this argument with you."

"Fine, fine. Do you still intend to name your firstborn Luke?"

"Hard yes. Do you still want to travel around the world in a speedboat?"

"To be fair, speedboats are awesome, and if it were possible to get around the world in one, I would probably do it. But yes, I still want to travel the world, though I'm open to other forms of transport now." I hide a smile behind another bite of pizza. "Do you still sleep with that ratty old stuffed mouse?"

Felix turns his face away from me, and I burst out laughing.

"What, really?"

"It's not like I fall asleep holding it or anything," he mutters. "It's more just, you know, *there*, on my bed, when I fall asleep. It's practically a family heirloom, Jas, it belonged to my grandpa, so it's not like I'm going to throw it away, and it'd be disrespectful to shove it in a drawer or something, so—"

I hold up my hands. "Hey, no judgment here. This is a safe space, and all manner of sleepytime stuffed animal friends are allowed."

His gaze darts suspiciously in my direction. "Do you still sleep with one?"

"No, but I did for a long time, and there's no shame in that. This is a shame-free zone, I promise."

"Hm."

"Anyway, guess we're back to me again." I hesitate, not sure I want to dampen the mood with a heavy question, but I do genuinely want to know. "Do you still wish you'd been born into a different family?"

Felix goes quiet, and the silence stretches for long enough for me to regret asking. Then he lets out a breath in a slow hiss of air. "Not really, I guess. I'm not saying my parents are perfect, but they've been pretty okay to me the last few years. And they never made me feel weird about everything that happened, you know. Back then. They've been pretty supportive."

I stare down at our joined hands, his long, thin fingers nestled against my shorter, stubbier ones. "Are you going to tell them? About us, I mean."

"I kind of already did."

I stare at him, and he laughs.

"Don't look so shocked. I told them last night. I mean, not everything. But I told them I'm gay, and there's a boy I like, and you know what? They were *relieved*. Turns out they've been worrying all this time about how I've been 'repressing' how I really feel. The subject only came up because Mom mentioned at dinner that I looked happier and seemed more like myself than I have in a long time, and I realized it was true, so I told them."

I squeeze his hand. "I'm so proud of you, Felix. Seriously, I can't believe how much you've done in, like, a *very* short amount of time."

"Yeah, well. I had a lot of time to make up for, I guess." He places his empty plate on the coffee table before turning to face me. "And speaking of making up for lost time…"

He leans in to kiss me, and I'm about to let him, but I pull away instead. "My dad's gonna be home pretty soon. We probably shouldn't."

The confused hurt in his eyes morphs into understanding. "Sure, I get it." He flops back onto the couch, comfortable and relaxed and probably not thinking I'm acting weird. Which I'm not. At all. "Wanna watch something until he gets back? Maybe something with fewer angsty teens and more space battles?"

I lower myself onto the cushion next to him, and it really does feel good when his arm slides around my shoulders. "Yeah, sounds good."

Chapter Sixteen

"Well, boys, I hope you saved me some—"

Dad freezes in the living room doorway, his gaze traveling from me to Felix and back again. The pizza box and our empty paper plates lie forgotten on the coffee table, and before my dad announced his presence, Felix and I were drowsing on the couch with our arms around each other, my head on Felix's shoulder and Felix leaning in to press a kiss to my forehead.

"Um," I say. "Hey, Dad. Didn't hear you come in."

Dad is in his usual gaming gear, wearing a white tee with "What Doesn't Kill You Gives You XP" printed across the front, faded blue jeans, and his favorite pair of ratty red sneakers. The car keys still dangle from his fingers, and his eyebrows lift behind his black-rimmed glasses.

"Hello," he says. It's a neutral word said in a neutral way, but I know I'm in danger.

I get carefully to my feet and gesture for Felix to do the same.

"Uh, so you remember Felix?"

Dad frowns, and I can practically see the complicated mathematical formulas spinning in his head as he studies the soccer god in front of him. "Felix from fifth grade? Didn't he and his family move away?"

"They did. Turns out they moved here. Funny coincidence, huh?"

"Yeah." Dad's eyes narrow as he studies us. "Funny."

In desperation, I grab the pizza box and flip it open, sending the tempting scents of cheese and roasted vegetables wafting toward Dad's nostrils. "We saved you some pizza."

Dad doesn't even glance at it. "Most kind."

Felix nudges me with his shoulder. "I should probably get going."

"Right, yeah, of course. I can drive you home—"

"No, it's okay," Felix says. "I'm only a few blocks away. I can walk."

Glad for an excuse to escape the storm cloud of Dad's disapproval, I escort Felix to the front door. I'm just opening my mouth to apologize when he ducks in and plants a goodnight kiss warmly to my lips.

"You didn't expect me to leave without doing that, did you?" he asks.

The front door has barely closed behind Felix when a throat clears behind me. I jolt and spin around, and Dad is standing there with a paper plate stacked with pizza and a stern set to his jaw.

"So I think maybe we need to have a talk?" he says.

I sigh and follow him into the kitchen.

****

In the end, it's not as bad as I fear. Once I spill the whole story about what happened in fifth grade and my quest to make things right, Dad is significantly less wary, more so when he learns the whole situation has the Cam seal of approval.

"Dad, honestly, sometimes I think you like him more than you like me."

"Cam is a very nice boy," Dad protests, dabbing

pizza sauce from his chin with a torn-off piece of paper towel. "And really, I thought if you'd end up locking lips with anyone in our living room, it would be him, so this whole Felix thing has kind of thrown me for a loop."

I almost choke on my water. "Me and Cam?"

Dad quirks a brow as he meets my eyes. "The two of you just seem *very* close…"

"Yeah, because he's my best friend."

My brain does some bizarro revisionist history and imagines it was Cam, not Felix, who I was with tonight. Cam with his arms around me, Cam's lips against mine. I want to laugh at the ridiculousness of the idea, but my throat is suddenly dry. Must be all that salty pizza.

Dad shrugs and pops a mushroom into his mouth. "Anyway, if Cam approves of you and Felix, then I have no complaints. Except"—he holds up a finger—"there will be absolutely no having Felix over when I'm not home, and your bedroom door stays open at all times when the two of you are in there together."

My face heats up. "*Dad.*"

"I'm serious, Jasper. I know you're a teenager, and you probably have lots of…feelings, but you're too young to be thinking about sex. Well, you're too young to be having sex, anyway. When I was your age, I definitely thought about it a *lot*. But I didn't do it, and neither should you."

I press my hands over my face and contemplate throwing myself out the nearest window. "Dad, ugh, why—"

"I know for you and Felix there's no risk of anyone getting pregnant, but STDs are still a real concern. If the two of you ever decide to be intimate with each other, it's important to get tested and always remember to wear—"

"Okay, nope, I'm leaving." I lurch out of my chair and cross the room in three long strides. "Off to bed now, good night!"

I've just shut my bedroom door behind me when Cam texts me to ask how things went tonight. My fingers hesitate over the screen, and I go with a highly descriptive "fine" before launching into the mortifying tale of my dad trying to talk to me about "being intimate." When I mention my face is probably still somewhere in the tomato range shade-wise, Cam's response is immediate.

—*this i must see.*—

I snap a quick selfie and send it to him. There's a pause, dots appearing and disappearing.

—*you don't look like even a distant relative of the tomato family. anyway, I can leave you alone if you're trying to sleep.*—

I rearrange the pillows I'm reclining against and hide a yawn behind my hand.

—*i'm not. not tired yet. how about you?*—

My screen fills with a selfie of Cam on the couch with his three-year-old brother Davy fast asleep on his chest.

—*kind of trapped right now. mom will be home around 11, so i guess i just have to hold out until then.*—

I zoom in on the picture. It's a little grainy because of the low light, but Cam's hair looks soft and fluffy like he's just washed it, and he's wearing a gray hooded sweatshirt and plaid boxer shorts. Davy is in his pajamas, the blue ones with little red trains that seem to be his favorites, and his face is so angelic it's hard to remember this is the same kid who once dumped an entire plate of spaghetti on his mom because his meatballs were "too round."

It's an adorable freaking picture, and it's an effort to tear my eyes away from it long enough to type a response.

—you could just wake him up. tell him to go to bed.—

—no freakin way. i'd rather live on this couch for the rest of my life than deal with waking this kid up. you think the spaghetti incident was bad? try waking davy up from a dead sleep.—

I grin.

—that bad, huh?—

—i'd tell you to try it and find out, but i like you too much to condemn you to an early grave.—

We text a little more about random stuff after that, until around 11:05.

—mom's home. looks like i'm finally free!—

—isn't she going to have to wake davy up anyway to put him to bed?—

—nah, she's got that magic mom touch. she can get him upstairs and into bed without waking him up. heck, one time she put him into his pajamas and brushed his teeth and he never even opened his eyes. but me, i so much as breathe wrong and he's awake and screaming. she's a wizard, i tell you.—

We trade goodnights, and I'm still smiling as I set my phone back on the nightstand and switch off the lamp. Right before I drift off, it occurs to me that Felix hasn't texted me since he got home, and I haven't even thought about texting him. And then sleep sweeps in like a tide and washes the thoughts away.

Chapter Seventeen

I catch up with Raven before class the next morning. She's at her locker with Lars, and as usual, I feel seriously underdressed in their company. While I'm wearing my usual T-shirt, hoodie, jeans, and sneakers combo, Raven is rocking a satiny green dress cinched at her waist with a length of white ribbon, and Lars has on a loose white button-down, slate-blue tie and a pleated blue skirt paired with fishnet stockings and the usual boots.

"Hey." I lean my shoulder against the locker next to Raven's. "Did you get my texts yesterday?"

I know she did, but opening a conversation with *"Why didn't you reply to my texts?"* is never a good look.

She frowns into the distance for a comically long moment before she snaps her fingers. "Oh yeah, sorry! I meant to reply, but then I got busy and forgot."

She turns back to her locker and devotes herself to the important business of fiddling with her magnets. I exchange a glance with Lars, who shrugs.

"So, uh, what are you going to do?" I ask.

Raven gives the trans flag magnet one final twist and pushes the locker door closed. "About what?"

"About Jess? Look, obviously it's none of my business, but she really seemed worried about you, and I got the impression she knows you like her and, I don't know, maybe feels the same way?"

Raven goes still, and I snap my mouth shut. Jess was definitely putting out major signals, but what if I misunderstood?

Raven recovers from her momentary freeze and draws herself to her full height. "Look, the truth is…I've decided to give up on Jess."

I gape at her and turn to Lars, who shakes their head with an unmistakable sense of "no comment."

"What do you mean, you're giving up on her?"

"I've been thinking about it," Raven says, smoothing out her dress even though it's already picture perfect, "and it doesn't make sense to get into a relationship right now. We're in our senior year, and even if she did like me, we'd only have a few months together before we graduate, and then we'd either have to break up or go long distance. Who needs that kind of stress? So I'm just going to give up on her and focus on getting decent grades and helping with the QSA, and everything will be fine."

"Before you ask," Lars says to me, "I've already pointed out that this is idiotic and makes no sense."

"It's not idiotic," Raven says.

Lars makes an "eh" sound and rocks their hand back and forth.

"Okay, well, even if it is, it's what I'm going to do." Raven sighs and leans her back against the lockers. "Look, I'm just tired of this, okay? I'm tired of feeling miserable, I'm tired of getting my hopes up, I'm just *tired*. Please just trust me when I say that this is what I want to do, okay?"

Lars takes Raven's hands in both of theirs. "Babe, of course we trust you. But trusting you and thinking you're making a huge mistake are two different things."

Before Raven can respond, a wolf whistle splits the air, and Tyler, Mac, and Muncher saunter into view with their usual entourage of chortling teammates.

"Aw, Barbie and Henry, holding hands," Tyler says with a sharp laugh. "You two freaks finally figure out nobody else is gonna want to go out with you?"

Muncher chortles, which seems to be what he's best at when he's not stealing other people's sandwiches, but Mac just rolls his eyes and keeps scrolling through his phone.

I scowl and open my mouth to say something, but Raven shakes her head. Tyler and his goons keep walking, and soon they're out of sight down the hallway, probably looking for someone else to torment.

"It's not worth it," Raven says quietly.

Lars folds their arms. "I wish they'd stop calling you Barbie, though. Transphobia and homophobia are one thing, but xenophobia, too? It's like they're trying to fill out an intolerant jackass bingo card or something."

At my confused look, Raven explains, "It's because my last name's Abarra. Guess that was a little too exotic for someone like Tyler, so he started calling me 'Barbie' back in eighth grade."

I shake my head in disgust. "That guy's such a tool."

"They all are," Lars says. "All those guys on the soccer team."

I almost say something, but in the end, I keep my mouth shut. There's nothing I can say to convince Raven and Lars that Felix is different than the rest of his friends, and that's okay. That's something he'll just have to prove to them himself.

****

The ticket booth that day is more crowded than

usual.

"So how long have you been gay?" The girl leans in with elbows on the table and wide, sparkling blue eyes fixed on Felix.

Felix blinks at her. "Uh, all my life? That's kind of how it works."

"Oh right, right, totally."

Another girl pipes up, "My cousin's gay. He took his boyfriend to prom last year. Are you guys going to the homecoming dance together? Because that would be super cute."

Felix's eyes dart in my direction. "Well, I haven't asked him yet, but I'm kind of hoping we will, yeah."

The two girls erupt in a loud, "Aww!" and I consider sliding under the table and hiding until all of this is over.

Over the next fifteen minutes, we're visited by half the cheerleading squad, a delegation from the student council, and a group of guys from the basketball team who fist-bump Felix and all say some variety of, "You never seemed like somebody who'd be into dudes, but at least that means Hailey's free now, hur hur." Mac and Muncher filter in after that, acknowledging my existence with a curt nod and a "Hey" before regaling Felix with the questionably hilarious tale of how Muncher made the boys' toilets overflow this morning.

After what seems like an eternity of popular guy meet and greets, the crowd filters off to lunch or wherever they're supposed to be right now, and Felix and I are left alone. I breathe a deep sigh and sink back against my chair.

"Sorry about all that," Felix says. His hand finds mine and squeezes, and I manage a weak squeeze in return. "I guess word kind of got around, huh?"

"Yeah, just a little."

"Everybody seems pretty cool with it, though. With us, I mean."

My stomach twists, and I force a weak smile. "Yeah."

"Hey…" Felix's fingers tighten over mine. "Are you okay?"

I'm not. I keep thinking about Lars and Raven in the hallway this morning, Tyler's voice dripping with disgust as he called them "freaks." It makes me so mad I can hardly speak.

"It's just weird," I manage. "How well everybody's taking this."

Felix shakes his head, understandably confused. "Did you want them to not take it well?"

"No, but this isn't how it usually goes, is it? When people at school find out you're queer, they don't just smile and act like it's all great and fine and cool. You get bullied. You get comments in the hallway and people being jerks about it."

Felix's voice is cool. "Yeah, I'm pretty sure I know what that's like."

"Right, exactly. You know how this usually plays out. I'm not saying I want people to treat us differently now they know we're together, but this big, friendly welcome… It's only happening because you're popular, and something about that rubs me the wrong way."

Felix's fingers go still in mine. He carefully pulls his hand back and drops it into his lap.

"What exactly do you want me to do?" His voice isn't cold, but it isn't warm, either. "Tell everybody to stop being okay about this? Ask the guys to call me names and beat me up behind the bleachers?"

"No, of course not. I don't want people to start treating you like crap. I just wish they could be this nice to every queer kid at school, that's all."

We sit in a stormy silence for a bit, and then Felix lets out a soft breath.

"Do you think it would help if I joined the QSA?"

My heart gives a little leap. "Do you want to?"

His shoulders lift in a half shrug. "I always wanted to, but to be honest, I'm not sure they'd want me there. I haven't exactly been nice to the queer kids in this school. But maybe if I started going to meetings and, like, spending time with the people there, they wouldn't get picked on so much. Maybe I can stick up for them like…" He sighs. "Like nobody ever stuck up for me."

He doesn't mean it as a jab at me, but I still feel a twinge of the old, aching shame. I reach across the distance between us and take his hand.

"I think that'd be really great. We have a meeting today after school if you want to come?"

He ventures a small smile, and when he leans in to kiss me, I let him.

"I was serious about the homecoming dance, you know," he says. "I do want to go with you. If you want to go with me."

I knock a pen off the table and have to spend a second searching the floor for it. My voice echoes in the space under the table as I bend to retrieve it. "Yeah, of course I do."

"Well, good then. Because I really want to dance with you."

I sit back in my chair, slightly breathless with the rescued pen in my hand. "You know I can't dance, like, at all."

"Neither can I. I thought we could figure it out together. And I also thought that maybe…you'd want to be my boyfriend. Or let me be yours, or however this works." He gives a nervous chuckle and ducks his head. "Yeah, um, I'm not very good at this. But what do you think? About the whole dancing and being boyfriends thing, I mean."

I imagine us dressed in suits and swaying together to some sugary sweet love song, Felix gazing lovingly down at me, the word "boyfriends" tied around us like a red ribbon. It's something I should want. I *want* to want it.

I squeeze his hand. "Yeah. Let's do it."

****

Felix's hand is tense in mine as we step up to room 215.

"It's gonna be okay," I tell him.

"It might not be," he says. "But it's my fault if it's not. I won't blame them if they don't want me here."

I give his fingers an encouraging squeeze. "Let's just see how it goes, okay?"

Felix takes a deep breath, and I push open the door.

I was afraid it would be one of those bad-guy-enters-the-saloon moments from old westerns where everything goes dead silent and the whole place *stares*. Thankfully, that doesn't happen. The desks are in their standard semi-circle, and most of the QSA members are sitting in them or milling around talking to their friends. I catch some furrowed brows here and there as Felix and I enter, but no one shouts abuse at him or orders him to leave. Lars isn't here yet, at least. So far, so good.

Our luck doesn't hold. By the time we sit down at a pair of free desks on the far side of the room, all eyes seem to be on us, and more than a few people steal dark glances at Felix as they whisper to their friends.

Felix is like a statue beside me, his face chiseled in stone, his hands clasped so tightly the knuckles are turning white. When a voice from across the room says, "What's he even doing here?" Felix mutters something like, "Maybe this was a mistake," and starts to get to his feet.

And suddenly Cam is there, giving Felix a companionable pat on the shoulder that keeps him in his chair.

"Hey, I'm so glad you guys could make it!" Cam's pink polo shirt has a little embroidered pig on the pocket, and that plus the khaki pants makes him look like someone's friendly uncle on casual Friday. "Thanks for coming!"

Felix peers up at him with a healthy amount of suspicion and says nothing.

"No soccer practice today, then?" Cam asks with a friendly lift of his eyebrows. "Or did Jasper convince you to skip?"

Felix casts a nervous glance in my direction, but he finally answers in a low voice. "No, no practice for the rest of the week. For homecoming."

"Makes sense. Well, since you're new here, you don't have to do anything but observe today. But if you want to help out with any of the projects or events we're doing, let me know. Or actually, let Raven know. She's the real boss around here."

"You've got that right." Raven steps up beside Cam, and there's only a slight hesitation before she smiles at Felix. "Cam and Jasper tell me you want to join the QSA?"

Felix shifts uncomfortably in his chair. "Yeah, if… I mean, if I can, I'd like to."

"You definitely can. We could always use new members." Raven lifts her voice so it cuts through the whispers from other parts of the room. "And everyone here is super nice, so I'm sure they'll do their best to make you feel welcome. We all know what a big step it is to come to one of these meetings for the first time." She turns to Cam, her voice dropping to a normal level. "You ordered the food, right?"

Cam opens his mouth, closes it again, and then turns his back on us as he pulls his phone out of his pocket. He starts tapping furiously on a food delivery app while Raven grins and rolls her eyes.

"Seriously, where would you guys be without me?"

"Hungry and very disorganized," I say.

Raven laughs and heads off to talk to someone else, and Felix and I are left on our own for the time being.

When I glance around the room, the mood seems to have warmed a bit. There's no more whispering, and the few glances that find Felix seem more curious than hostile.

I rest my hand on his arm. "You doing okay?"

His jaw is still tight, but he looks a little less like he's going to bolt for the door any second. "Yeah. I think so." His voice drops to a murmur, just loud enough for me to hear. "It's just been a long time since I've felt like this. Like people are talking about me, and not in a good way. I know I deserve it after how I acted, but I guess it's bringing back some stuff I'd rather not think about."

I wrap both my hands over his and hold them tightly. "Look, if you need to leave, just let me know, okay? But I really think this is going to be all right. The people here

139

are really cool, and once they get to know you, they're going to like you just as much as I do."

Before he can reply, someone swears, and I jerk my head to find Lars in the doorway. Their gaze goes from Felix's face to mine, and I manage a wincing smile but can't quite meet their eyes. Lars frowns deeply and heads for a chair on the other side of the room, and I hope for the hundredth time that this will all somehow turn out okay.

When the meeting starts, Raven gets us sorted into our respective homecoming-related groups. I'm with Cam, Lars, and the rest of the float group, and Felix sits next to me and watches in silence as we chatter about decorations and what music should be blasting from our float as it trundles down the parade route. We've just decided on a medley of disco songs from the '70s, partially inspired by my glorious rainbow pantsuit, when Lars arches a slender blond eyebrow in Felix's direction.

"Guess we won't be seeing you up on that float with us, huh, Morales?"

Felix blinks and opens his mouth, but Cam swoops in with a faint frown on his face.

"No one has to do anything they're not comfortable with here, Lars. You know that."

"I'm just saying," Lars continues, coolly but without malice, "it's easy to walk around holding some guy's hand when you know nobody's going to say anything about it. But if you wanted to actually do something to show you're on board with the QSA? You could be on our float. Or help out with literally any of the other homecoming events we're doing. But that would mean standing up in front of everybody and showing them you're one of us, and I don't think you want to do that, do you?"

There's a heavy silence afterward, not just from our table, but from the rest of the room, too. Even Cam seems at a loss for words, something I'd previously thought impossible.

And Felix, instead of fleeing the room or going into a full-on panic attack, stares calmly back at Lars and nods.

"You're right."

Lars blinks.

"You're right," Felix says again. "I was a prick to you and a lot of other people for a long time, and that wasn't okay. I don't have an excuse, not one that would matter, anyway. All I can say is I want to do better. And if that means being on this float with you guys or doing whatever else I can to help the QSA, then I'm in. Just tell me what to do, and I'll do it."

Lars stares at him for a long time, and I hold my breath.

Finally, some of the ice melts, and Lars uncrosses their arms. "Well, it's a start. And if you're serious about being on the float, we're going to have to find you a costume."

Felix shoots an uncertain glance in my direction, but he still nods.

A little more warmth enters Lars's expression. "Don't let Raven help you find something, though. You'll be there all day." Their voice drops to an echoing stage whisper. "Love her to death, but she's a little bit of a *perfectionist.*"

"I heard that!" comes a stern voice from across the room.

Lars calls, "Love you, Rave!" and our table erupts

in laughter. When I glance over at Felix, he's smiling, too. He catches me looking and takes my hand where it rests on the desktop, his fingers taut but slowly relaxing. We trade warm smiles, and I squeeze his hand.

Lars lets out an exasperated breath. "Ugh, you guys are annoyingly cute. Fine, Morales, I guess I can give you a pass if Jasper thinks you're all right. But one crack about my skirt or the way I talk, and I'll rescind my goodwill. You've been warned."

"Actually, I like your skirt," Felix says. "I've always thought your outfits look really cool."

Lars narrows their eyes, but Felix gazes back at them unblinking, radiating sincerity.

"Yeah, well," Lars mutters, "if that's actually true, then thank you. And if you really do like my style, maybe I can help you find something to wear on the float."

Felix gives a dazzling smile I'm surprised doesn't knock Lars right out of their chair. "Yeah, I mean, if you don't mind, that'd be great."

Our group settles back into float-related discussion with no further altercations. As the talk turns to the best places in town to purchase rainbow streamers, my attention shifts to Cam, who has been oddly silent. His gaze is fixed on Felix and my joined hands, his brows knitted and his lips pressed tightly together. When he catches me watching, he offers me a sunny smile and shifts his attention to Lars, but there's a new tension to his posture that doesn't go away. Cam doesn't glance our way again, but I draw my fingers back from Felix's so I can grab a pen and jot a few meaningless notes in my notebook. Felix drops his hand into his lap, and I spend the rest of the meeting ignoring the knot twisting in my stomach.

Chapter Eighteen

"You know you don't have to do this," Cam says.

I bump his shoulder with mine. We've just started up the walk to his front porch, and it's a chilly, perfect night with a velvety stretch of sky and stars above us. "You said that already."

"I know."

"Like, three different times."

He laughs. "I know. I just want you to know it's okay if you want to back out. Especially if you've got other plans or something."

"What other plans would I have at seven o'clock on a school night?"

He turns his back on me as he wrestles his keys out of his pants pocket. "You know. With Felix."

The words are light, but uneasiness settles like a stone in my stomach. I give a weak attempt at a chuckle. "Just because we're sort of going out doesn't mean I need to spend every waking moment with him." It didn't even occur to me to see if Felix wanted to do anything tonight after the QSA meeting—it was just a given I'd be spending the evening with Cam. "Anyway, I was promised pizza if I helped you babysit, and no way I'm going to pass that up."

Cam laughs, but it doesn't sound as bright and easy as usual. He starts to slide the key into the front door lock, but I stop him with my hand on his arm.

"Cam, are you okay?"

His eyes widen for an instant before he flashes a puzzled grin. "Um, yeah, why?"

"You just seem… I don't know. You know you can talk to me, right? About anything."

His gaze drifts to where my hand rests on his arm. He's only wearing a light hoodie over his pink polo, and I can feel the heat of his skin through the thin layers of fabric.

I pull my hand back and stuff it into my pocket.

The motion jars him out of whatever he was thinking about, and he gives a normal Cam smile as he unlocks the front door. "We better get inside. Alice has probably had about as much of Davy as she can handle."

We find Alice stretched out on her back like a starfish on the living room carpet, groaning in the general direction of the ceiling. Davy is mashing all his fingers onto the keys of his toy piano in a rhythm that sounds vaguely like "Jingle Bells," and the resulting noise is probably my karmic punishment for the off-key trombone torment I put Dad through when I was younger.

"Oh thank God," Alice says when she sees us. She stretches one arm weakly in our direction. "He's been doing that for forty-five minutes, and he screams every time I try to get him to stop."

Cam leaps into action, grabbing Davy around the waist and swinging him up into the air. Davy squeals and yells, "Cammy, Cammy, I wanna be an airplane!"

Cam readjusts his grip on Davy, but before he swoops his little brother up into airplane position, he shoots me a look that clearly says, *Get rid of the piano*. I hurry over to it while Davy is giggling madly and being flown around the room, and soon the musical torture device is safely stowed on the highest shelf in the living room closet.

Alice has fled by then, and I don't blame her. Luckily, Cam is an expert at distracting Davy, and before the kid has even noticed the vanishing piano, Cam brings out the magnetic blocks and asks Davy what he wants to build. Davy seeks my input with all the seriousness of a forty-five-year-old business magnate discussing his next real estate development plans. We eventually decide to build a rocket ship, a house for dogs to live in—*not* a doghouse; Davy is very firm about that—and a green pepper. Cam nods like these are perfectly rational design choices, and we set to work.

It ends up being pretty fun. For all that Davy is the king of tantrums in his darker moments, he's also a bright, funny little kid I don't mind spending time with. Still, I know my role here. I'm the support. I order the pizza, I clean up the blocks after Davy gets bored of them and Cam detours him to a box of puzzles, and when it's time to put Davy to bed, I fill his sippy cup with water and arrange the stuffed animals on the bed according to their owner's strict instructions.

Once my job is done to Davy's satisfaction, I settle into the plush blue armchair in the corner of the room. Cam has tucked Davy in so snugly I doubt the kid can even move his legs, but Davy looks warm and happy, a little smile on his face as he cuddles his stuffed frog and gazes adoringly up at Cam. Cam sits on the edge of the mattress with a book in his lap, and when he opens it to the first page, I see the cover has a picture of a muscle-bound tiger in a tank top with a bespectacled turtle cowering beside her.

"Once there was a tiger named Tilly," Cam begins, and I relax into the lulling tones of his voice.

It turns out to be a basic tale of unlikely friends—the sporty tiger and the nerdy turtle becoming besties in this case—but there's a warm humor to it that touches something deep inside me. Or maybe it's just the way Cam reads it.

I find myself staring at Cam as the story goes on, which is completely acceptable since he is, after all, reading a story. And while I look at him all the time, every day, this is one of the rare times when I feel like I'm actually seeing him.

He doesn't have Felix's chiseled jaw or Tyler's sultry blue-green eyes, but his face is kind and open, with soft, rounded features and warm dark eyes. He's overdue for a haircut, so strands of silky black hair tease the tips of his ears and trail past his eyebrows. Every now and then he reaches up to brush back a strand of hair, and it promptly falls right back to where it was before.

But more than how he looks, what really draws me to Cam is who he is, what he is. He's the kind of person who always wants to help, even if it hurts him. The kind of person who would ignore his own feelings if it meant making a friend happy. The kind of person who tucks his little brother into bed and reads him stories and never looks like it's an imposition or like he has better things to do.

Davy is firmly asleep by the time Cam finishes the story, and after closing *Tilly Tiger and Tabitha Tortoise,* Cam leans down and kisses his little brother gently on the forehead. Davy stirs a bit but stays asleep, and as Cam brushes the hair back from the contented little face, there's so much tenderness in his expression it makes my heart ache.

It's in that moment I realize I love him.

****

Cam leads me down the hall to his room, where I have to clap my hands over my mouth to keep myself from yelling.

Cam's bedroom is clean. There are no clothes on the floor—I can actually see the carpet—and there isn't a water glass or a teacup in sight. All the books are back in their proper places on the bookshelf, the bed is made, and even the desktop is tidy. A piece of paper sticks halfway out of one of the desk drawers, but other than that, the place is immaculate.

"When did you have time to do this?" I demand.

Cam drops onto the edge of the bed with a bounce. "Last night when you were hanging out with Felix. I figured I might as well use my time doing something constructive, so I cleaned the place up."

My chest aches a little at the thought of Cam all alone tidying his room while I was curled up on the couch with Felix. "Well, you did a great job. Just never let my dad see this, or he'll be on my case to get my room looking this good."

"I don't think there's much chance of your dad ever having a reason to be in my room. But if the worst happens, I promise to come help you clean."

And he would, wouldn't he? He would drop everything and come help me, just because I needed him.

I hesitate, then sit next to him on the bed. "You know I'd still like you even if you didn't help me all the time, right?"

He shoots me a quizzical frown. "Yeah, I know that."

"And even if you weren't happy sometimes, and if sometimes you didn't feel like laughing and joking and stuff. I'd still like you, Cam."

"Okay…" He shakes his head. "Where is this coming from?"

"I just want you to know you can be real with me. If there's something you want to say, or something you've been feeling, you can tell me. You don't have to pretend everything's okay when it's not. Or that you're not…feeling things when you are."

His eyes widen, but he doesn't run away or change the subject or do anything but gaze back at me.

"Oh," he says softly.

We sit in silence for a few beats, and then he lets out a long breath.

"How long have you known?"

I stare down at my hands, not because I don't want to look at him, but because I'm afraid of what I might feel if I do. "Not very long. I mean, if I'm even right about…what I'm thinking."

"What are you thinking?"

If I'm wrong, this is going to be very embarrassing. But I still take a breath and force the words out. "That you like me. Like that."

There's a long silence.

"To be fair," Cam says quietly, "I never pretended I didn't."

The knowledge zings through me like an electrical current, leaving me stunned and breathless.

He gives a strained laugh. "Honestly, I thought you'd figured it out a long time ago. I mean, I flat-out told you I liked you the first day we met."

"Yeah, but I thought you meant as a friend."

"I did mean it like that. Sort of. But even then, I guess I liked you in a more-than-friends way." He falls backward on the mattress and presses his hand over his eyes. "I'm really sorry about this, Jasper."

"Why are you sorry? It's not like you did anything wrong."

"Ugh, but you're with Felix, and I didn't want you to feel awkward about this."

"The only reason I'm with Felix at all is because you helped me talk to him." I shake my head as the full weight of that fact hits me. "You liked me the whole time, but you still helped me with Felix, a guy who *bullied* you. Why did you do that?"

He peels his hand away from his face and shakes his head at me. "Because you said you liked him, and I wanted you to be happy."

With anyone else, I might doubt their sincerity, but I know Cam means every word. Tears prickle my eyes, and I blink them away furiously.

"God, why are you like this? Why are you so…so…"

He laughs weakly. "Stupid?"

"Amazing." My voice is thick with emotion. "You're so amazing, Cam."

The words crackle between us, and my mind flashes to Felix. It's meant so much to see him coming back to himself this week, taking such huge, fearless steps toward living an honest life that makes him happy. What would it do to him if things didn't work out between us? How can I even think about breaking his heart after everything I did to him when we were kids?

"Look, Jasper…" The mattress shifts as Cam sits up. "The whole reason I never told you about this was because I didn't want it to change anything between us. Because yeah, I like you as more than a friend, but that doesn't mean I can't be happy being friends with you." His voice drops, and there's a soft, ragged edge to it. "I don't want to lose you."

That snaps me out of my brooding. "You're not going to lose me. I promise."

"Really? Because you look kind of freaked out right now."

"I am. But not… It's not because you like me." I meet his eyes, and another tremor goes through me at the realization that we're alone in Cam's bedroom, sitting together on his bed with barely any space between us. "I don't want to lose you, either."

Cam's hand lifts, hesitates, and then wraps over mine. He's done it a dozen times before, but this time I really feel it—the heat and solidity of his fingers, the steadiness of his pulse thrumming against my palm. I stare at our clasped hands and wonder what it would feel like to slide my thumb along his skin or to bring his hand to my heart and hold it there.

I swallow. "I should probably get home."

His hand slips away from mine. The bed rocks as he gets to his feet, and I pretend I'm not disappointed as he moves away from me.

He walks me to the front door, and we hover there awkwardly before I give him a quick, back-patting hug. "I'll see you tomorrow, okay?"

He offers a tight-lipped smile as he steps back from me. "Yeah. Drive safe, okay? And thanks for helping out tonight. I owe you one."

"You already paid me in pizza, remember? We're good."

A faint line forms between his eyebrows. "Are we?"

"We are," I say. "I promise."

As I step out into the chill of the night and the front door closes behind me, I draw a slow, shaking breath and hope I'm telling the truth.

Chapter Nineteen

The next morning, I find Felix waiting at my locker. He's scrolling through his phone with his back to the wall, dressed in a snug maroon hoodie and green cargo pants. The easy smile teasing his lips makes my stomach twist with guilt.

I really do care about him. What happened between us pretty much shaped my whole life up to now, so it makes sense for this to be an endgame kind of situation, two long-lost friends who once shared a kiss now reunited and in love.

So why do I keep thinking about Cam?

Felix's eyes light up when he sees me, and he tucks the phone into his pocket. "Hey, Jas." He leans in to kiss me, and I hate that I turn my head so he catches my cheek instead of my lips.

"Hey." I manage a smile as I spin my locker dial. "Don't you usually hang out with the soccer guys in the morning?"

Felix shrugs and slides his hands into the front pocket of his hoodie. "Yeah, but I wanted to hang out with you instead." He hesitates. "If you're okay with that."

"Yeah, of course I am!"

Silence falls between us as I try to convince my brain to identify the correct books to stuff into my backpack.

"Uh, so how was your night last night?" I ask.

Felix shrugs again. "Not bad. You?"

Cam's hand in mine, electric tingles shooting up my arm, the cold knot of disappointment as his fingers pulled away...

I choke on a cough and swing my locker shut. "Yeah! Um. It was okay."

A bang from down the hall stops any further conversation, and I turn just in time to see Lars staggering away from where they've collided with a row of lockers.

"Whoops." Tyler Bruce is smirking, and the blonde girl on his arm looks way too amused. "Sorry, Henry, my bad."

Lars rubs their shoulder and glares at Tyler. I'm just thinking I should go over and see if they're okay when Felix marches past me and straight up to Tyler.

"What's your problem, man?" Felix sounds calm, but his shoulders are tense, his jaw tight. He positions himself in front of Lars, forming a protective wall between them and Tyler.

Tyler's smug smile drops at the sight of Felix, but he rolls his eyes as he answers. "It was an accident, dude, calm down. Anyway, I barely touched him. He probably just tripped over his high heels."

The girl, who I've finally realized is Hailey, Felix's ex-girlfriend, laughs loudly, and Lars's cheeks go pink. They're not even wearing heels, just chunky black boots that frankly look awesome paired with dark purple leggings, a black skirt, and a Nirvana T-shirt, but of course that doesn't matter to freaking Tyler Bruce.

Lars recovers enough to throw a cool look at Hailey. "Please, you wish you looked as good as me in heels."

Tyler takes an angry step forward. "What did you say to her, you skirt-wearing freak?"

Felix doesn't back away, and he and Tyler end up practically nose to nose.

"That's not okay, man." Felix's voice is clear and strong, the embodiment of the confident soccer captain. People all around the hallway stop to watch. "You've gotta stop treating people like this. It doesn't make you look cool. It just makes you look like an ass."

Without waiting for a response, Felix turns his back on Tyler and faces Lars. "Hey, Jasper and me were gonna go grab a soda before class, you wanna come?"

Lars's mouth opens and closes without sound for a second. "Sure?"

Felix rests his hand on Lars's shoulder, and they walk away from Tyler and Hailey without a backward glance.

I'm still gaping when they reach me, but I manage a nod of greeting at Lars. "Hey. Your shoulder okay?"

Lars blinks a few times but eventually nods. "Yeah, it's fine. Look, Felix…"

They're clearly about to thank him, but Felix waves it away before Lars can get the words out. "Come on, let's go get those sodas. First bell's gonna ring in a few."

Lars shoots me a stunned look, but I just smile and shrug as the three of us head for the soda machine. When I glance over my shoulder, Tyler is still standing in the same spot, hurt and confusion creasing his tanned brow while Hailey taps her foot impatiently. Felix starts asking Lars about costume ideas for the parade float, even making plans to meet up during a study hall they have in common to talk about it. He never seems to notice that all eyes in the hallway are locked on him, including mine.

****

Even with our soda machine detour, I slide into my desk in first period a few minutes before the bell rings. Cam bounds in a few seconds later, looking flushed and cheerful with the usual little yellow container of his mom's pastries in his hand. He beams at me as he drops into the seat next to mine.

"Hey!"

I will not be awkward, I will not be awkward.

"Hey!" My voice cracks on the word, and I wince.

Perfect. I am the king of normal.

Cam kindly does not comment on my voice's journey to the upper register, so I dig the coffee thermos out of my backpack like usual and hand it over to him. He pours half of it into his travel mug and then hands it back to me, also as per usual. But when he passes me a red bean bun shaped like a panda, he does it without our fingers touching, carefully letting go of the pastry before the warmth of his hand can brush against mine. Which is fine, of course.

The rest of the morning is also fine, Cam and I talking and laughing like always as we go through our classes, but I can't help noticing he hasn't touched me once. He doesn't put his arm around me as we walk down the hall—our shoulders don't even brush—and he doesn't grab my hand, pat my shoulder, mess up my hair, or do any of the other little physical things I've gotten so used to. When he sits next to me on the bleachers at the start of gym class, there's a noticeable space between us. And when he starts bouncing his knee while telling me a funny story about Davy, it never once bumps into mine.

By fourth period, my body is practically aching with

how much I want him to touch me, and I'm starting to wonder if I'm losing my mind. He drops his pen midway through the lesson, and I bend down to pick it up before he's probably even registered it's fallen. He blinks in surprise as I hold the pen out to him, and even though he tries to avoid my hand, I shift my grip at the last second so his fingers land on mine.

He freezes, eyes going wide, and mumbles an apology as he sets the pen carefully on his desk.

I turn back to my textbook and drop my hand into my lap. My skin is on fire where Cam touched me, and my heart pounds in my ears like we've just done way more than exchange a chaste brush of fingertips. *What the hell is wrong with me?*

The problem is that I know. I know what's wrong with me, and I have no idea what to do about it.

****

I'm weirdly relieved when lunchtime rolls around, and I'm back at the ticket table with Felix. He shows up with Lars in tow, both of them so deep in conversation they don't even seem to notice I'm sitting there at first.

"Just because I dress like this doesn't mean I don't like sports," Lars is telling Felix in a dry, amused voice. "I played soccer for years, and I was good at it, too."

Felix's smile is bright and open, a lot like the one I remember from when we were kids but wider, more confident. He's looking at Lars with a level of interest and delight I haven't seen on his face during any of our own conversations. "You're right, I shouldn't have assumed. So if you were so good, why'd you stop?"

Lars's expression darkens. "Let's just say the locker room isn't the friendliest environment when you look like me."

Anger flares in Felix's eyes, bright and brittle and unforgiving. "That's not okay. Look, if you ever want to play again, just let me know, all right? I know we're a few weeks into the season, but I'm sure Coach'll make an exception, and I'll make sure nobody bothers you. Even if you don't want to join the team, we can just kick the ball around sometime or something. I mean, if you want."

Lars blinks a few times and gives a cautious shrug. "Yeah, that might be fun. I mean, if it wouldn't be too embarrassing for you, getting your ass handed to you by somebody in a skirt."

"Are you kidding? Half the girls' soccer team could probably kick my ass. You'd just be the latest in a long line of skirt-wearers to be better than me at soccer."

Lars shakes their head. "You keep surprising me, Morales."

"It's Felix," Felix says.

Lars readjusts their grip on their bookbag strap and ducks their head to hide a smile. "I better get to Chem. Ms. Stievers will have me cleaning out all the test tubes with a toothbrush if I'm late again. See you at the meeting later?"

"Absolutely," Felix says. "You still have to help me find a costume, remember?"

After Lars disappears around the corner, Felix drops into the chair next to me, and I bump my shoulder gently into his. "You two seem to be getting along pretty well."

He gives a little start and glances at me. "Yeah, I guess we are. I didn't realize we had so many classes together, and h—They're really cool. Sorry, I'm still getting used to the pronoun thing. But yeah, I never thought I'd have so much in common with…" He winces

157

and looks away.

I keep my tone gentle. "With someone like Lars?"

Felix stares down at his lap. "Yeah. Which is a pretty awful thing to think, isn't it? Just because they like to wear a certain kind of clothes doesn't mean they're a completely different species or something. They're just...Lars. A really cool person I never would've even considered talking to before. Guess I'm really not any better than Tyler."

He looks genuinely torn up about it, so I rest my hand on his arm. "The difference between you and Tyler is you figured out what a tool you were being and took steps to change it."

He waves a dismissive hand.

"I'm serious, Felix. You went from closeted and homophobic to a freaking champion of the QSA in a few days. This time last week you were afraid to even look at me because someone might think you were gay, and now you're holding my hand in public and standing up to your best friend for Lars. That's not nothing, man."

He gives a *whatever* kind of shrug, but his lips curve into a small smile. "I guess."

We sit in silence for a little while, organizing the remaining dance tickets and getting ready for our thrilling final day of sales, before Felix clears his throat.

"He's not, you know."

I glance at him. "Hm?"

His gaze is fixed on the tickets he's counting, but the warmth in his eyes is unmistakable. "Tyler. He was never my best friend. I've only ever had one best friend, and it was you."

Affection and sadness tangle inside me, and I give his arm a playful nudge. "Was?"

"Well, I wouldn't call what we're doing now being friends, would you?"

My smile fades, and I'm glad he's not looking at me. "Yeah, I guess not."

****

The rest of the day sails by, and before I know it, Felix and I are on our way to room 215 to work on the final prep for homecoming. Felix doesn't need to hold my hand as we approach the meeting this time. His steps outpace mine, and the second he walks into the room, Lars greets him with a wave and a gesture at the empty desk next to theirs.

It seems like word's gone around about Felix standing up for Lars earlier because everyone has a smile or a kind word for him, and there's no hint of the chilliness they were directing at him yesterday. My steps slow to a stop by the doorway as Felix slides into a chair and falls into conversation with Lars.

There's something magnetic about Felix, and more than a few of the QSA members look at him with open admiration, like they want to impress him or at least be noticed by him. I wonder if this is the side of him the soccer team has been seeing all this time, the reason they made him their captain in the first place.

He and Lars are already laughing about something, and I can't deny it feels good to see Felix so animated. We talk and smile and hold hands, but I don't really see this side of him. Whatever Lars has just said has him practically in hysterics, and it's great to see that light in his eyes, even if I'm not the one who put it there.

A warm shoulder bumps into mine, and I jump.

I turn to find Cam smiling gently down at me. His arms are full of take-out boxes, and I hurry to relieve him of a few before the QSA's dinner ends up on the floor.

I help him get the food arranged on the table at the front of the room, and we're nearly done by the time I realize we haven't said a word yet.

"So what's on the menu today?" I ask.

Cam pulls a stack of paper plates from a box under the table and sets them near the food. "Just sandwiches. We may have had a complaint or two about the Thai food last night being 'too spicy for human consumption.' "

I laugh. "Not gonna lie, I barely ate any of it because I was holding out for pizza at your place, but I did see smoke coming out of a few people's ears."

Cam scratches the back of his neck. "I guess my spice tolerance is pretty high. Mom's been feeding me spicy curries since I was little. Said she wanted to prepare me for 'a life of culinary exploration.' "

"That is a very your-mom thing to say."

We both laugh, and things feel normal for a second. Then the moment fades, and Cam clears his throat.

"Well, I better…" He gestures in Raven's direction.

"Yeah! Of course, go for it."

He hurries off, and I lean my back against the edge of the table and sigh.

Raven starts the meeting, and once we've separated into our event-related groups, Lars and Felix head off to the costume room while the rest of the float committee nails down the final details of our performance. Since said performance mostly involves us dancing around and throwing rainbow necklaces at the crowd, it doesn't take too long to get things finalized, and I'm left with nothing to do but wander down to the costume room to see how Lars and Felix are doing. Raven is about to do it herself, but she has way too much on her plate already, which

I'm starting to suspect is a desperate attempt to distract herself from the Jess situation, so I volunteer instead.

The costume room is in the stuffy space underneath the stage, accessible by an old wooden door that looks like a good breeze could knock it down. The door is propped open when I reach it, and as I slip into the room, low voices drift to me from the maze of costume racks.

"—really my style," Felix is saying with a self-conscious attempt at a laugh. "I don't think I'm the right type to look good in something like this."

"Please, are you kidding?" Lars's voice is dry but sincere. "People are gonna fall over when they see you."

"Because they'll be laughing so hard?"

"No, because you look so…"

There's a short silence.

"What?"

Lars huffs out a breath. "Don't pretend you don't know."

"Know what?"

"That you're *hot*, stupid. This whole chiseled jaw, sulky pout thing you've got going, and the biceps, and just the whole freaking thing, okay? You're hot. It pains me to say it, but it's a fact, and I'm not going to pretend it's not true. You could stand on that float wearing a potato sack, and everybody'd still go nuts over you. But as it happens, this outfit looks amazing, and nobody's going to laugh at you because they're all going to be too busy trying not to combust from how hot you look in it. So."

There's a pause, and then I hear Felix's voice, softer than usual. "Oh. Well…thanks."

"No problem," Lars says gruffly. "Now, you asked me in here as your style consultant, and it's my

161

professional opinion you should wear this outfit on the float. Are you going to listen to my professional opinion, or are we going to have words?"

"No words necessary. I'll wear it."

"Good." A forced lightness enters Lars's voice. "Should we go show your boyfriend what you're wearing, or do you want it to be a surprise?"

The aforementioned boyfriend slips quietly back toward the door.

"Maybe we let it be a surprise," Felix says.

I back out the door and slip down the hallway. Instead of heading back to the meeting room, I detour to the drinks machine and end up sitting in the stairwell sipping orange soda and trying not to think too hard about anything. I've nearly finished the can when the door opens behind me, and someone settles down next to me on the steps.

"Do you have some kind of Jasper tracking technology I don't know about?" I ask.

Cam smiles and gestures at the stairwell door. "I saw you through the glass. I was on my way to get some poster board from the art room." He lets the silence stretch for a moment before he glances at me again. "You okay?"

My shoulders slump. "I don't know. Everything's kind of a mess right now."

Another silence, this one heavier.

"Because of me?"

I turn to him so quickly I'm surprised I don't get whiplash. "No! No, it's not you, I promise. I'm just... I guess I'm realizing what I always thought I wanted might not actually be what I want, and it's kind of hard to deal with."

A faint frown creases his brow, but he nods. "You want to talk about it?"

I do. But once I say the words out loud, there'll be no going back.

"Maybe later. For right now, could you just sit with me? I mean, if the poster board isn't too much of an emergency."

He smiles. "I think they'll survive a little longer without it."

He folds his hands in his lap like he's preparing to stay for a while, and before I can second-guess myself, I lean into him, resting my head on his shoulder and letting the side of my body slide into place against his. He freezes at first, but then his arm slides around my shoulders, and he leans his head against mine.

I close my eyes and breathe out a soft, relieved sigh.

We're close enough that I can feel the slow in and out of Cam's breathing, so I feel it when he exhales a breath that trembles a little. He doesn't say anything, and neither do I. We just sit and hold each other, and my mind goes blissfully quiet for a while.

After a few minutes, Cam shifts. "We should probably get back."

I don't want to move. I want to stay here, possibly forever, and pretend nothing exists outside the warm safety of this moment.

"I know," I say. "Just one more minute." *Please*.

Cam goes still, the arm wrapped around my back tightening a little. "Okay," he whispers.

Chapter Twenty

After the meeting, Cam, Lars, Felix, and I walk out to the school parking lot together. Felix and Lars talk animatedly about nicotine cravings, as apparently Lars used to smoke but quit last year, while Cam and I walk quietly together a few steps behind them.

It's a gorgeous fall night, cool but not cold. The air has that great October crispness to it that makes me think of pumpkins and trick-or-treating and the hayrides Mom and Dad used to take me on when I was a kid. When I glance at Cam, he's watching me, and I choke out a self-conscious laugh.

"What? Is there mayo on my face?"

He shakes his head. His hands are stuffed in the pockets of his jacket, and the cool evening light makes his eyes seem darker than usual, deep black pools glittering with reflected starlight.

"So I was thinking," he says, "that I might go to the dance after all."

I beam at him. "Really?"

"Yeah. Raven said she wanted to go but didn't have a date, so we figured maybe we could go together."

It's incredible how quickly this news deflates my good mood. It genuinely feels like someone has punched me in the stomach. "Oh. I thought Raven was…I mean, I didn't know that you guys…"

"As *friends*, Jasper." Cam rolls his eyes and gives

me a playful nudge with his shoulder. "Raven's a lesbian, and I don't like her like that anyway."

Just like that, I'm smiling again. "Oh. Okay."

"Anyway, did you want to get ready together? Mom said I can have the car, so we can go pick up Felix and Raven and all head to the dance at the same time."

"Yeah, sure! I mean, I'll check with Felix, but that sounds good."

"What are you checking with me about?" Felix asks. He and Lars have paused about ten steps ahead of us.

"About the dance," I say as Cam and I close the distance between our two groups. "Cam and Raven are going together, and he said he'll drive us if we want."

Felix gives a light shrug. "Sure, works for me." He glances sideways at Lars. "Are you going to the dance?"

Lars shakes their head, a soft twist of disappointment on their face. "Nah. Nothing to wear, and I hear it helps if someone actually asks you."

Felix frowns. "Well, I'm asking you. I mean—" He makes a sweeping gesture that includes himself, Cam, and me. "—we're asking you. You should go with us. We'll be a group."

Lars's gaze flits over to me. "I wouldn't want to be a fifth wheel."

"You won't be," I say. "Seriously, you should come. If you want to, I mean."

"You should." Felix's voice is warm and firm. "It'll be fun. I promise."

Lars looks like they're about to refuse, but Felix keeps gazing at them with big, hopeful brown eyes, and they release a grudging breath. "Fine, I guess I could go. But I wasn't kidding about not having anything to wear."

"I'll help you find something," Felix says. "It's only

fair. You helped me find a costume for the float."

Lars's eyes widen. "You don't have to do that."

"No, I want to. Anyway, the mall's still open for another two hours. That's plenty of time to find something. You don't mind, do you, Jas?"

I startle at the sound of my name and shake my head. "No, of course not. Go for it."

Lars shoots me a wary glance, but I offer the friendliest smile and thumbs up I can manage. They and Felix head for Felix's car, falling into easy conversation as they go. I feel Cam's eyes on me and find him watching me again, a look on his face I can't decipher.

"Still need a ride?" I ask.

Cam nods, and we head for the edge of the parking lot where I parked the clunker.

"Are you really okay with that?" he asks as I unlock the car.

"Hm? What do you mean?"

He shakes his head and climbs into the passenger seat. I slide into the driver's seat and pull my door closed with the usual *creak-slam*, and we sit in the quiet closeness of the car.

I slip the key into the ignition but don't turn it, and the seconds tick by.

Cam lets out a soft breath. "I'm having kind of a hard time figuring you out right now."

I wait for him to say more, but he doesn't. I should probably say something myself, but the words stay locked inside.

Finally, Cam throws me a crooked smile. "You know, I hear it helps if you turn the key."

I give a weak breath of a laugh. "Sounds weird, but let's give it a try." The engine roars to life with only a few alarming clinks and clanks. "Wow, who knew?"

The silence that falls between us is unusual, and even more unusual is the fact that Cam doesn't turn on the radio. We drive along the cool blue streets with no sound but the rattling of the car around us.

We pull up to Cam's house a little while later, and I slide the car into park in his driveway. The car clicks and clanks as it settles, but Cam doesn't move. He stares out the front windshield, his lips pressed together and his brow creasing. I'm starting to wonder if I should say something when he turns to me.

"Do you ever want to do something, but you're scared of what might happen if you do?"

Everything in me goes still. My mouth is suddenly dry, and it takes a moment to find my voice. "Um. Sometimes, I guess?"

"I mean, I think I'm pretty good at reading people. I can usually pick up on what's going through people's heads, especially if I know them pretty well. But there's always the chance I'm just seeing what I want to see. That I'm wrong."

His eyes lock onto mine, dark and questioning in the dimness. The breath catches in my throat.

"Am I wrong?" he whispers.

I stare at him. I shake my head.

He swallows. "That's what I thought."

He doesn't move for a long moment. Then he reaches across the distance between us and strokes his fingers lightly down my cheek.

I let out a trembling breath and close my eyes. His fingers leave a warm, tingling trail along my skin, and I want to grab his hand and clutch it to me. Kiss it. Kiss him.

When I open my eyes, Cam is watching me closely. He's drawn his hand back and isn't touching me anymore, but I'm aware of the heat of his body next to me, the fact that he'd only need to lean a very little way to press his lips to mine.

But he doesn't. He turns his back on me and opens the car door.

"See you tomorrow, Jasper."

And then the door closes behind him, and I'm alone.

Chapter Twenty-One

The homecoming parade is due to start at ten a.m., but everyone participating is expected to get to the school early to get everything ready. I show up to the float prep area in the back parking lot a little after seven, knowing I probably look like hell, but that's what happens when you stay up half the night staring at your bedroom ceiling. Luckily, some kindly soul on the student council got the school to spring for a breakfast spread, and among the donuts, muffins, and fruit are several insulated drinks dispensers labeled "coffee."

I make a beeline for the nearest one and fill a paper cup to the brim. There was no time to get my usual caffeine fix from home this morning and definitely no time for breakfast, so I pile baked goods onto a paper plate with one hand while cradling my coffee with the other.

"Jasper?"

It's Raven. A blue bandana nestles in her voluminous curls, and it's strange to see her wearing casual clothes, just a loose-fitting sweatshirt and skinny jeans paired with worn blue and white sneakers.

She frowns as she studies my face. "Are you all right?"

I slide on my sunglasses. The morning sun isn't all that bright, but maybe they'll hide the dark circles under my eyes. "Just didn't sleep well. Luckily, coffee exists."

When I manage a vague approximation of a reassuring smile, Raven reaches past me to grab a paper cup of her own. "Well, let me know if you need some ibuprofen or something. And if you're not feeling up to being on the float, I'm sure we'll be okay. Everybody's probably just going to be staring at Felix, anyway."

Honestly, she's not wrong. Our float would probably still be a success even if Felix were the only one on it, though I doubt he'd be a fan of that idea.

"How's the prep going?" I ask.

Raven's aquamarine nails hover over a blueberry muffin, then swerve for a donut instead. "I mean, we literally just started, but so far, so good. There's a lot to do, what with hanging up the streamers and signs and getting the sound system hooked up and everything, but we should be able to manage it. And we have an extra worker since Felix is here, so if you feel like finding a quiet spot and taking a nap or something…"

A nap sounds like literal heaven, but if I sleep now, I'll be like a zombie for the parade, only way grumpier and probably less hungry for brains.

"Thanks, but I think I'll be okay."

Raven shrugs. "I'm just saying, it's gonna be a long day. First the parade, then the fair, then the dance. If I were half dead with sleep deprivation, I'd definitely consider grabbing a nap if I had the chance."

"I'll think about it." I throw her a teasing smile. "Are you done mothering me now?"

She smirks. "Watch it, Sinclair. This is one mother you don't want to mess with."

"Oh believe me, I know it."

She heads off with her coffee and donut, and I find a quiet corner near the buffet tables to sit and press my back against the cool brick of the school building. The lot is filled with floats and people, but I've purposely been avoiding looking for anyone I know, two people in particular. I can't hide forever, but I need a little more time before I can face either of them. And it probably wouldn't hurt to get some food and caffeine into my system, either.

The table shields me from most prying eyes, and I drink half my coffee and nibble through most of a donut before a flicker of movement catches my eye.

Cam is standing about ten feet away, stock still and staring at me. He's wearing a hooded blue sweatshirt and jean shorts with sneakers, and the sight of him makes my stomach flip in a not-unpleasant way. Before I've figured out whether or not I'm ready to talk to him, he crosses the distance between us and drops down beside me.

"Are you, um…" His gaze burns into the side of my face, but I keep my eyes on my breakfast. "Are you okay?"

I give a humorless laugh. "Sure."

Concern is radiating from him now. I can practically feel it warming my skin. "Really, though."

"I'm fine. I just didn't sleep well last night."

"Oh."

I wait for him to ask why I didn't sleep well, but he doesn't. Probably he already knows.

"So…" he says, "have you seen Felix yet?"

I shake my head and take another sip of my coffee.

"He was asking where you were. Raven said she saw you over here, and maybe you weren't feeling so hot, so I came to investigate."

"Mm."

"Jasper, would you look at me, please?"

I glance at him.

"Okay, but for longer than that, and get rid of the sunglasses."

With a sigh, I pull off the dark glasses and look at him properly. He looks tired himself, and his hair sticks up in the back like he didn't comb it this morning.

"Good," he says. "Now, can we talk about this?"

"About what?"

He gives me a flat look.

I groan and lean my head back against the wall. "You're the one who left."

"Because things were going in a very definite direction, and I didn't want you to do anything you'd regret."

"Isn't that for me to decide?"

"Probably. Usually. But you've been going through a lot lately, and I wasn't sure if…"

"If what?"

He lets out an exasperated breath. "If you wanted to kiss me because of me or because of Felix."

I blink. "What?"

"Look, I get it, okay? You've been in love with Felix since you guys were little kids. You went through all this to have another chance with him, and now he's blowing you off to spend time with Lars. It makes sense that you'd be jealous, and that you'd want to do something to get back at him."

I am robbed of the power of speech for a few seconds. "Is that what you think? That I'd kiss you to get back at Felix?"

"I don't think it's something you consciously decided to do, but…"

I start laughing. It might sound a little unhinged, but

I guess that comes with the territory of being ridiculously sleep-deprived. "Cam, no. That's so, so not what was going on." I shift my body so I'm facing him, the remains of my donut forgotten on the plate in my lap. "I don't care that Felix is hanging out with Lars. That's what's been making me feel so weird because I should care, right? If I really want to be with him like that, I should mind when he starts spending a lot of time with somebody else. But I don't."

Cam looks like he, too, has momentarily lost the ability to speak. His mouth opens and closes, but before he can say anything, Raven is standing in front of us squinting into the sunlight.

"I hate to interrupt, guys, but we need to get started. Jasper, are you going to take the sane option and grab a nap, or are you going to ignore my very wise advice and stay awake instead?"

Escaping into dreamland for a while is a tempting idea, but I shake my head. "Your advice is very wise, as always, but I really think I'll be okay. And if I collapse from exhaustion, just work around my unconscious body."

She glances skyward and holds up her hands. "Don't say I didn't try. All right, in that case, I want you helping Felix and Lars with the decorating, and Cam, I'm pretty sure you're the only one who remembers how Eric showed us to hook up the sound system last year, so..."

Cam throws her a salute as he crawls to his feet. "I'm on it, chief."

"That's vice chief," she says as she walks away.

Cam hesitates, then holds his hand out to me. I let him lift me to my feet, and neither of us lets go right away.

"We're talking more about this later," he says.

I nod, and he squeezes my hand before releasing it. The warmth of his fingers lingers on mine as we follow Raven to the float.

****

Despite Raven's advice and my better judgment, I stick with my decision to stay bravely awake. To aid in my pursuit of remaining conscious, I pour myself another cup of coffee and fill it with enough sugar to probably make Dad consider disowning me for real. Once the sugar-caffeine combo kicks in, I'm able to find the energy to help decorate the float and exist as a reasonably sociable individual with Felix and Lars.

"Wait, wait, wait." Felix turns to Lars so quickly he drops the streamer he was holding. "You've never seen them? Like, not any of the movies? Ever?"

Lars shrugs as they drape a rainbow streamer over the side of the float. Their fashion is more subdued today, just jeans and a tie-dyed sweatshirt with their usual boots, white-blond hair pulled up in a ponytail. "Nope. How many are there, like two or something?"

Felix's expression is a complicated blend of disbelief and growing determination. He draws a bracing breath. "Right, we're fixing this."

Lars lifts an amused eyebrow. "Are we?"

"I'm serious. Are you busy tomorrow?"

"No…"

"Then you're coming over to my place, and we're watching at least the original trilogy." He looks sharply at Lars. "Tell me you at least know who the main character is."

Lars makes a show of furrowing their brow. "Is it that ugly green alien baby thing?"

Felix groans and clutches his head in his hands, and Lars and I both start laughing.

"Felix, I'm pretty sure they're messing with you," I say.

Lars presses a hand to their chest like an offended Southern belle. "Mess with Morales? I would never."

Felix's eyes narrow. "So you do know? This is *very important*, Lars."

"Of course I do. It's William Shatner, right?"

There's a long moment of silence.

"I don't think words can express how much that hurt me," Felix says.

Lars laughs again. "I'm sorry, it's just too easy." They finish adjusting the sign on the side of the float that says "Nelson Springs High Queer Straight Alliance" and drop their arms to their sides. "Look, Morales, I didn't want to have to tell you this, but the truth is…we're Trek folks in my family. The biggest rule in our house is that Trek is superior to all other space-based franchises, no question, no argument."

Felix's mouth opens and closes without sound for a few seconds.

"But you haven't actually seen any of the movies," he says.

"No."

"So then how can you know for sure?"

Lars's lips twitch. "Well, I guess I can't."

Felix's jaw sets in fiery determination. "Today after the parade, we'll start watching the original trilogy—we can finish it tomorrow, and maybe watch the prequels if there's time."

"Fine." Lars heaves an exasperated sigh I'm pretty sure is all for show. "But there better be snacks. And I

175

reserve the right to throw in a few episodes of Next Gen if I get too bored of laser swords and *pew-pew-pew*."

"What's Next Gen?"

Lars rests a solemn hand on Felix's shoulder. "Clearly I have much to teach you."

The two of them are smiling at each other, streamers—and me—forgotten, when Felix blinks and shifts his gaze over to where I've been watching all of this transpire.

He gives a strained smile. "So what do you think, Jas? You up for a movie marathon?"

A flicker of disappointment crosses Lars's face, but I'm already shaking my head.

"Nah, I'm good," I say. "I don't want to get in the way of Lars's education."

Palpable relief from Lars, and honestly, Felix looks a little relieved, too.

"You sure?" he asks.

The funny thing? I really am.

"Completely."

We get back to decorating, and my eyes keep tracking over to Lars and Felix as I work. It's hard not to notice the effortless way their conversation flows, the way Lars manages to constantly tease laughter out of Felix with their dry humor, and really, just how happy and at ease both of them look with each other. At one point, Lars drapes a rainbow streamer over Felix's chest like a sash, and Felix grins and reciprocates by creating a rainbow headband for Lars. It settles lightly over their pale hair and somehow stays in place even as Lars dances along to the music Cam has finally managed to get pouring from the float speakers.

Felix shoots Lars an amused smile but doesn't dance

himself, at least not until Lars takes hold of both of his hands and shakes them around playfully. Felix laughs and protests, but pretty soon Lars gets him to actually dance, and predictably, he looks *good*. I'd bet Felix has never danced before in his life, but it seems to come as naturally to him as soccer does.

And some of that is Felix's natural grace, but most of it is Lars.

It just makes sense, Felix and Lars. Everything between them is so easy and natural, like these are two people who were always meant to be in each other's lives.

I know what that feels like.

But maybe Felix doesn't, because he still catches my hand and squeezes it when he passes me, and he drops a kiss onto my cheek before he heads to the buffet table to get a muffin with Lars. Guilt floods through me, and I stare after him wondering if I'm just seeing what I want to see, if I want so badly not to hurt him that I'm imagining he has feelings for Lars. Because if we both like someone else, then no one gets hurt if we break up, right?

Against all odds, we get the float decorated and ready to go, and then it's time to put on our costumes and wait for the signal to move out. A flutter of nerves hits me as we head to the costume room. For all that I have lots of other things on my mind right now, it's still not enough to drown out the burst of stage fright that accompanies the thought of everyone in school seeing me in a snug rainbow pantsuit.

But Raven is looking stressed and telling us to hurry, so I push away my nerves, grab my costume, and duck behind the nearest privacy screen to get changed. When

I emerge, everyone else is already dressed, and Raven is painting a rainbow flag and a pansexual pride heart on Cam's cheek. Felix is seated a few feet away while Lars leans over him, sliding a black eyeliner pencil expertly along Felix's lower lids.

"I promise, it's going to look great," Lars says. "We'll add just a touch of eye shadow to make your eyes really pop, and it'll be perfect. Trust me."

Felix swallows nervously, but he still closes his eyes so Lars can dab on a smoky gray-green.

"There," Lars says. "You're done. What do you think?"

Felix approaches the full-length mirror on the wall, and his eyes widen.

He looks amazing. His eyes are dark and soulful under the careful eye makeup, and the outfit Lars picked out for him is perfect, a sheer black top and sparkly gold pants paired with a rainbow boa and white sneakers decorated with pride stickers. Lars also put some product into Felix's wavy brown hair to make it look fuller and softer, and it's definitely doing its job.

"Well?" Lars sounds a little nervous, and Felix immediately smiles.

"I never thought I'd say this, but I love it."

A pleased flush comes to Lars's cheeks. "Well, you should, because you look fantastic."

"So do you." Felix gestures at Lars's rainbow tee, black leggings with jean short-shorts, and high-heeled black boots. Lars's flush deepens to a full-on blush, and I wonder if they might be about to spontaneously combust.

Raven finally spots me hovering in the background and snaps her fingers at me. She's still in her sweatshirt and jeans as she'll be out of sight driving the float, but there's a rainbow on her left cheek and a trans flag on her right. "Jasper, you're up next. We don't have much time, but I want to at least get a few rainbows painted on your face before we have to go."

Cam gets to his feet to give me his chair, and I notice his outfit for the first time.

He throws me a sheepish grin as he holds out his arms. "What do you think?"

I shake my head, at a loss for words.

It is, essentially, pajamas. It's a rainbow onesie with a hood, and it looks so velvety soft I have to resist the urge to run my fingers over it, or maybe test its softness by throwing my arms around Cam and hugging him tight.

"It's perfect," I say. "But aren't you hot?"

He lifts an eyebrow, and I laugh.

"I mean, temperature-wise. Aren't you kind of warm in that?"

"Oh absolutely. But this is the noble sacrifice I make for the QSA."

My eyes widen, and I step forward so I can better examine the bear ears I've just noticed on top of Cam's hood. "Wow. Okay, you need to put the hood up."

"Jasper, I'm already burning up in this thing."

"Just for a sec. I need to see. For science."

He flips up the hood, and I discover that Cameron Matsumoto-Rogers in a rainbow hood with bear ears may be the cutest thing I've ever seen in my life.

"Okay, well, you look adorable," I say. "And wait, wait, don't tell me… Turn around."

Cam sighs deeply but does so, confirming my suspicions.

There's a fluffy cotton ball of a bear tail on the back of the onesie.

"Oh my God. Cam, you have a *tail*."

Before I can decide if I dare give said tail a friendly squeeze, Raven catches my arm and steers me to the vacant chair. When I blink at her in surprise, she rolls her eyes affectionately and starts dabbing paint on my cheek.

"You can flirt with him just as easily while I'm painting your face," she says in an undertone. At my stunned look, she grins. "We are on a schedule, after all."

Chapter Twenty-Two

The QSA float is the hit of the homecoming parade. We creep along behind floats packed with cheerleaders, the student council, the A/V club, the drama club, and various other school organizations, but ours is the only one with blasting disco music and Pride Parade energy, and ours is definitely the only one with Felix Morales dancing on it in sparkly gold pants.

An actual cheer goes up from the students lining the street when Felix starts dancing, and the rest of us take the hint and let him take center stage. He looks a bit overwhelmed at the attention at first, but the energy of the parade and the music is hard to resist, and soon he's dancing and waving his arms around like a pro. As the more rhythmically challenged members of the float squad, Cam and I are the ones who toss the beaded necklaces at the crowd, and before long, half the students along the parade route are decked out in rainbow beads.

Dread coils in my stomach as we approach a bunch of guys from the soccer team, but they cheer for Felix louder than anybody, and when Cam and I throw beads at them, they swing them over their heads and chant, "Morales, Morales, Morales!" So I guess there won't be any egg-throwing today.

I vaguely notice Tyler isn't with them, but then we're moving on to the next part of the parade route, and I have a new batch of cheering people to assault with pride merch.

The parade lasts about forty-five minutes, taking us on a slow circuit of the neighborhoods around the school. Some people in the surrounding houses venture out onto their lawns to watch us pass, and while not all of them look thrilled to see a float full of dancing queer kids decked out in rainbows, most of them cheer and wave at us and gladly accept our beads.

By the time our float pulls back into the school parking lot, all of us are out of breath and sweating and laughing. Cam's got the sleeves of his onesie rolled up and is fanning himself with one hand, and Felix and Lars sit in the corner laughing about the girl who threw her underwear at the float—or more accurately, at Felix—about ten minutes into the parade.

I flop down next to Cam and enjoy the cool autumn breeze on my flushed face. My whole body is buzzing, and above all else, there's a feeling of euphoria racing through me that's unlike anything I've ever experienced. I used to think being gay would bring nothing but misery, shame, and hardship to my life, but today it brought me and a lot of other people joy, and that's pretty freaking amazing.

Cam nudges me with his elbow. "Well, newbie? What did you think of your first parade?"

"It was seriously amazing." I pluck at the stretchy fabric of my pantsuit. "But I still can't wait to get out of this thing."

Cam laughs and holds out the arms of his onesie. "Honestly, same. But I'm not gonna lie, I'll be sad to see the pantsuit go."

"It is pretty spectacular."

He shrugs. "I meant more how you look in it."

I gape at him. He holds my gaze for a few breaths and then averts his eyes, a small smile tugging at his lips. Before I can figure out what to say, the float shudders to a stop near the school entrance.

"All right, everybody off!" Raven shouts.

The homecoming fair has already started, colorful sales booths and food stalls filling the soccer field, but the thought of marching all the way up there and wandering through the bustling crowd doesn't appeal to me. After I change back into my sweatshirt and jeans, I look blearily around and finally spot the holy grail of the costume room—a worn old green couch that has probably seen more decades on this earth than my grandparents.

I flop onto it and close my eyes. I should set my phone alarm so I don't sleep for too long, but I'm too tired to do anything but tuck my arm under my head before I pass out.

****

A gentle shake of my arm wakes me, and I open my eyes.

Cam leans over me with a teasing smile on his lips. "He awakes."

I groan and haul myself into a sitting position, caught in that post-nap feeling of existing in an alternate dimension. There's a smear of rainbow face paint on my sleeve, and I don't even want to think about what my cheek looks like. "What time is it?"

"A little after three."

My mouth feels gummy and weird, and I'm sure my breath is less than delightful. "Three?"

"I guess you were tired." He pulls something out of his jacket pocket, and a carefully wrapped sandwich drops into my lap. "I saved you some lunch. There are chips, too, but I left them back in the QSA room."

I'm still sleepy and disoriented, but I shake it off as best I can. "Thanks. Is everybody else…"

"Most of them headed home already. Which we should probably do soon, too, but I figured you might want to eat something first."

Warmth fills me as I pick up the sandwich. "Thanks. Uh, is Felix…"

"He was here. I told him I'd make sure you were awake and dressed in time for the dance." His lips twitch. "He also apologized to me."

"For what?"

"For outing me to his friends, letting them bully me for months, all of that. He said you were the one who told him he should do it."

I sit up straighter, suddenly wide awake. "Oh. What, uh…what did you say?"

"I challenged him to a fight to the death, of course. We duel at dawn."

When I blink at him, he rolls his eyes and laughs.

"I told him I forgive him. I already told you, I got over all of that a long time ago. But I'm glad he wanted to apologize. Really, I'm just glad he's in a better place these days. He never seemed very happy before, but since you guys made up, it's been pretty clear how happy he is." His voice goes softer. "It's pretty clear how happy you make him."

I want to protest, but my stomach chooses that moment to remind me it's been subsisting solely on coffee and donuts today and requires real food ASAP. So instead of holding a half-asleep discussion on how I suspect my boyfriend is falling for someone else, I unwrap the sandwich and take a bite. Cam drops onto the couch beside me, and for a while I'm too focused on chewing to wonder what he might be thinking.

Then he clears his throat, and I realize he's been gathering the courage to speak since he sat down.

"Look, Jasper, I know we should probably talk about some things. But would it be okay if we just put all that on hold for a little while? It's not that I don't want to talk about it, but the dance is tonight, and you're going with Felix, and I just…I think you need to sort things out there before we, you know. Talk."

He's right, and I know it. But the thought still makes my stomach clench.

I close my eyes and drop my head into my hand.

"I know it's not going to be easy," Cam says in a soft voice. "But dragging things out isn't going to help anybody. Whoever you want to be with, and whoever you don't…you need to tell them, soon."

My voice comes out low and broken. "I don't want to hurt anyone."

I can't hurt Felix. Not when I finally got him back in my life.

"I know. But putting it off won't stop it from hurting. It might even make it worse." The couch shifts as he gets to his feet. "Raven said she'd give me a lift, so I'm going to head home. See you around five to get ready for the dance?"

I nod, and with one last bracing smile, Cam leaves me alone with my sandwich. I let it get soggy for a while, then toss it in the nearest trash can.

My bookbag is still up in the QSA room, so I head up there at a jog. The empty halls are oddly peaceful, but as I get closer to room 215, I hear the unmistakable sound of John Williams' soundtrack and the *pew-pew-pew* of laser fire.

"Okay, but why don't they just blast through that planet that's in the way?" Lars asks.

Lars and Felix sit against the far wall of the QSA room, shoulder to shoulder with a bag of corn chips between them and Felix's phone propped on his knee. The overhead lights are off, and I hesitate at the doorway, feeling like an intruder.

Felix pauses the movie with a tap of his finger. "It probably takes a long time to charge up enough energy to destroy a planet, so they wouldn't want to waste it on something that wasn't the rebel base. And they don't think the rebels can actually destroy them, so they feel like they can take their time."

"Okay, but they know the rebels have the plans and found a weakness, so I'm just saying…"

"They're in a huge battle station that can destroy entire planets." Felix gestures so emphatically he almost knocks his phone onto the floor. "Do you really think they're worried about the few beaten up old ships the Alliance managed to get together?"

"Well, we haven't watched the ending yet, but I'm pretty sure they should be."

Felix sighs out a laugh. "Look, do you want to watch the rest or not?"

Lars pops a corn chip into their mouth. "Yes, by all means, let's watch. I have no idea what might be about to happen, and I'm very worried our main characters are all about to get blown to bits."

Felix's fingers hover just short of touching the phone screen. "You know, we really don't have to keep watching if you're not into it. I know I said you *had* to watch, but if you're not having fun…"

"No, I am." The words come in a rush, Lars's eyes going wide. "I mean, we've made it this far. Let's keep watching."

Once Felix taps the phone screen to restart the movie, I take the opportunity to slip fully into the room. Felix and Lars jolt when they see me, but I wave my hand at them.

"Just here for my backpack. Don't let me interrupt."

"Did Cam finally manage to wake you up?" Felix asks. He looks like he's been jarred out of a dream, confused and off-balance as he blinks at me.

"Yeah. I'm gonna head home, but we'll pick you up around six-thirty, yeah?"

"Sure, sounds good." Felix hands the phone to Lars and gets to his feet. When he reaches me, he gives my hand a shy squeeze that makes my insides twist. "Remember, you promised to dance with me tonight."

I wrestle on a smile. "I know."

Lars is staring down at their shoes, their mouth set in a tight line. I want to be far, far away from here, so I stammer out my goodbyes. As I jog toward the stairwell, the epic conclusion of a decades-old space battle echoes behind me, but I feel like it's nothing compared to the battle going on inside me.

Chapter Twenty-Three

Cam's mom answers the door, takes one look at me, and pulls me into a crushing hug.

"Jasper, it's so good to see you!" She squishes me against her, then pats my cheeks so hard they sting. "Cammy's upstairs. Go on up and get ready for the dance, go, go!"

Some pretty intense shooing motions follow, so I slide past her and dart up the stairs. I nearly crash into Cam, who's just coming down.

He catches sight of my expression and laughs. "My mom?"

"She was pretty insistent I come up here *now*, so…"

"Mom, we have plenty of time!" he shouts down the stairs.

"I know, but I want to take pictures!"

Cam shakes his head and leads me down the hall to his room, which is still pretty tidy but not as pristine as it was the other day. A dark blue suit lies on his bed, and a few different pairs of dress shoes and socks decorate the floor. I carefully step over them and lift my suit from where I've had it draped over my arm in its plastic dry cleaning sleeve.

"Where should I, uh…"

Cam's gaze flickers from my suit to my face. "Oh, down the hall in the bathroom if you want privacy. Otherwise, you can get changed in here. I promise I'll turn my back."

It's such a weirdly gentlemanly thing to say that I want to laugh, but instead I just smile. "I'll go for the bathroom. Be right back."

It doesn't take long for me to get dressed, pulling on the gray pants, crisp white button-down, and gray blazer with its tailored lines and crimson pocket square. But I quickly encounter a problem when I sling the red tie over my neck.

I head back down the hall and push open the door to Cam's room. "So turns out I don't actually remember how to tie a tie…"

I'm faced with a Cam who is half in and half out of a pair of dark blue pants, shirt off and hair mussed. He blinks at me owlishly, and I quickly turn my back and face the hallway.

"Sorry!"

He huffs out an embarrassed laugh. "Jasper, it's fine. I should've locked the door."

"No, I should've knocked—"

"It's okay, really. And lucky for you, I'm great at tying ties, so I'll help you with that in just a sec."

I keep my back turned, listening to the rustling and occasional grunting of Cam getting dressed, and try not to think about the smooth skin of his bare chest or the fact that his boxers had little cartoon golden retrievers on them.

"All right, you're safe now," Cam says in a dry voice. "I'm decent."

I turn to find him fully clothed, boxers hidden beneath navy suit pants and surprisingly muscular chest tucked away under a standard white button-down like my own. His hair is still a little messy, and his cheeks are flushed, but he quirks a smile at me when our eyes meet.

"So didn't you wear a tie when we went to church?"

"Yeah, my dad tied it for me once two years ago, and I just never untied it." I hold up the red tie. "This one is new, and I forgot to ask Dad to do it before I left."

"Forgot?"

"It's possible I was just deeply ashamed."

Cam shakes his head. "All right, come here."

I step forward, and Cam knots the tie around my neck with gentle, efficient fingers. His face is all concentration, his lower lip trapped under his teeth as he works, and the whole thing is a lot more intimate than I was expecting. We're so close I can feel the whisper of his breath on my face when he exhales.

"There." He takes a step back. "Some of my best work."

I peer into the half-moon mirror over the dresser. The tie looks perfect, knotted beautifully and hanging at just the right length. "Wow, you really are good at this!"

Cam raises an eyebrow as he pulls on his blazer. "You doubted me?"

"Never."

I drop onto the edge of the mattress while he stands at the dresser mirror to tie his own tie. Somehow, he messes it up the first time and has to unknot it and try again.

I snort out a laugh but don't comment, and he throws a rueful look over one shoulder.

"So…" I say, "your mom said something about pictures?"

He gets the tie tied and turns around with a flush of success on his cheeks. "Yeah, she wanted a picture of me with my 'date,' but since Raven's not actually coming over here, Mom figured pictures with you would be the next best thing." His gaze skids away from mine. "I mean, if you don't mind. I know it might be kind of weird—"

"No, it's fine. Anyway, she seemed really excited about it. I get the feeling I'm not getting out of this house without having my picture taken."

"If you really don't want to, I swear she'll be okay with that."

"No, I don't mind. And it's kind of nice, actually. That your mom cares enough to want to take pictures of us like this, I mean."

Cam's expression softens, and I know he's thinking about everything I've told him about my relationship with my own mom. I try to imagine her looking on this night with the same level of enthusiasm as Cam's mom, or even the quiet, smiling support of my dad, but I can't envision it. All I can picture is the disapproving twist of her mouth, the hardness of her eyes as she looked at me.

Cam squeezes my shoulder. "Come on. We better get down there."

I try to force thoughts of my mom back to where they belong in the deep, dark parts of my brain, but they rush over me like a black tide and pull me under.

****

It's not that my mom didn't love me. But she never understood me, and that only became clearer as I grew up. When I was little, she was warm and easy with her affection. She'd wrap me up in a towel after my bath and dance me around the room, sit by my bed reading me stories in a mix of Spanish and English, kiss me on both cheeks and tell me how much she loved me a hundred times a day. But as I got older, things started to change.

The first time I noticed it was when I was around eight, and we were in Spain at some big family get-together at one of Mom's sisters' houses. There was a buffet of amazing homemade Spanish food, which I very much enjoyed, but the most interesting part of the day was getting the chance to play with my Spanish cousins, five of whom were around my age. We ran through the yard playing all kinds of games, but the boys started getting a little too rough, so I ended up having a quiet but honestly really fun time playing with two of my girl cousins and their dolls.

I'd just managed to communicate to them in my less-than-great Spanish that my doll was an alien who'd come down to Earth in search of the most delicious paella in the universe—"paella" being a word I'd just learned and was very proud of—when a hand wrapped around my arm and yanked me to my feet.

There was a visceral horror in Mom's eyes as she shook the doll out of my hands. It was like she'd caught me running naked through the yard or murdering a cute fuzzy animal or something.

"Jasper, what are you doing? Go play with the boys."

I frowned at her. "They're too rough."

"They're boys. They're supposed to be rough." She *shoved me, not gently, toward where my cousins were kicking a soccer ball around and taking every opportunity to tackle each other to the ground. "Go. Don't let me catch you over here again."*

I was puzzled and hurt, but I wandered over to the boys and made a few half-hearted attempts at kicking the ball. When Mom was occupied chatting with her sisters, though, I sneaked away and hid in the house for the rest of the party. Luckily, the boys decided to go on a walk around the neighborhood around that same time, so Mom figured my absence meant I'd gone with them. She hugged me when I wandered over to her some time later, and her flowery perfume filled my nose as she stroked my hair.

"There, now, didn't you have fun with your cousins?"

I nodded, and it wasn't exactly a lie.

I'd had fun with my cousins, just not the ones I was supposed to.

The next serious clash happened two years later when I was ten years old and best friends with an amazing kid named Felix.

I enjoyed drawing and always had, and I didn't let my lack of talent get in the way of churning out picture after picture of animals, buildings, cartoon characters, and people. Santa had brought me one of those fancy 64-packs of colored pencils for Christmas, and so I spent most of that afternoon lying on the living room floor sketching. At one point, Felix called, and we spent a good twenty minutes excitedly sharing what presents we'd gotten. But then he had to go, and I faced another empty page full of possibility.

A burst of inspiration struck me, and I grabbed the brown colored pencil and started to draw. When I was done, I held my creation up to the light. It was easily the best thing I'd drawn, a wobbly portrait of Felix that, while not strictly accurate or in any way good, definitely had a certain Felix-ness about it. I was sure anyone could look at it and know it was him, and I couldn't wait to tear it out of my sketch pad and show it to him.

I was still admiring it when I heard a "tsk" from

behind me, and I turned to see Mom watching me with her hands on her hips.

"Is that Felix?" she asked.

"Yeah! It really looks like him, doesn't it?"

She snatched the sketch pad out of my hands and stared at it for a while. "What's this?" She jabbed her finger at the page.

I craned my neck and gave an embarrassed laugh. "Oh, um, that's a heart."

"Why are you drawing hearts on a picture of Felix?"

She sounded upset, which didn't make any sense to me. "Because he's my friend and I love him."

Mom looked at me sharply. "You like *him. Someday you'll get married, and you'll love your wife, but you don't love Felix. You can't."*

Her voice was hard and flat, an absolute refusal. It reminded me of the hardness in her voice when she'd told me to stop crawling into her lap a few years earlier, that "big boys" didn't do things like that. Hurt stabbed through me, and I blinked back a sudden hot prickle of tears. "Why can't I love Felix?"

I was used to the anger on her face, but the disgust was new, a slow curl of her lip that cut me to my core. Shaking her head, she tore my drawing out of the sketch pad and tossed it into the fireplace. I watched the paper turn to ash and, again, got that sense that Mom was ashamed of me, that I'd done something she couldn't forgive.

"You don't love Felix," she said firmly, and when she handed the sketch pad back to me, I closed it and didn't draw again for a very long time.

When I told Dad about it later, he hugged me and

said I could love whoever I wanted, but Mom's words stuck with me. The shame stuck with me. And a few months later when Felix kissed me on the playground, I heard her voice echoing in my head, and it was her disgust I saw in the faces of the kids who pointed and laughed at us.

Chapter Twenty-Four

"Okay, that's good, that's good. Now this time, Cammy, you put your arm around Jasper, and Jasper, you put your arm around his waist. Perfect! Hold it!"

I plaster a smile onto my face and blink the spots out of my eyes as the flash goes off on Cam's mom's phone.

"Okay, now this time—"

"Mom, we really need to get going."

"Okay, okay, just one more, and then I promise you can go!"

Cam sighs, but he's smiling. For all that his mom has held us hostage to her camera for the last thirty-five minutes, she's so into it it's hard to get mad.

"Now, for the last one... Oh, I know, I know. Go stand by the fireplace. Yes, perfect. Now, Cammy, maybe you could put your arm around Jasper and kiss him on the cheek?"

Cam's face goes bright red. "Mom..."

"Oh honey, it would be so cute, and you two look so good together!"

"Jasper is dating someone *else*, Mom. I can't just kiss—"

"It's just for the photo, I'm sure his boyfriend will understand! He must see how good you two—"

"*Mom.*"

"It's fine," I say, both because it is fine and because I don't want this photo session to end in a nuclear detonation. "Friends kiss each other on the cheek sometimes, right?"

Cam's mom nods like I've delivered a divine message from above. "See? Jasper understands. This one's going in the Christmas newsletter for sure!"

Cam's eyes lock onto mine, and he murmurs, "Are you sure this is okay?"

An electric tingle shoots through my veins, and I nod. After one last waver of hesitation, Cam presses his lips softly to my cheek.

"Perfect! Hold it right there. I want to get at least five shots of this in case the first one doesn't turn out."

Cam manages to mutter, "Mom, oh my *God*," without lifting his lips from my face, and the movement tickles against my cheek and makes me laugh.

Pretty soon, we're both laughing, and rather than telling us off for spoiling the shot, Cam's mom keeps snapping pictures until we settle down. Then she steps forward proudly brandishing her phone.

"Well, if the café ever goes under, maybe I can get a job as a wedding photographer. Look at these!"

Her phone's photo album is full of artful shots of me in my gray suit and Cam in his blue one, but when she places the phone in my hand, my eyes zero in on the shot of Cam kissing my cheek. I'm just starting to laugh, and he's smiling, and we look so happy and natural together despite the unnatural pose that I swallow against a sudden rush of emotion.

I hand the phone over to Cam and take a few steps away to where Alice is keeping Davy occupied putting an animal puzzle together on the carpet. Davy is trying to jam a rooster into the giraffe spot, but he looks happy enough. Alice watches me with a small smile.

"She's right, you know." Her voice is low enough I doubt Cam can hear it. "You two do look good together."

I blink at her in surprise, and she grins.

"I might not have any interest in romance myself, but I know it when I see it. You two just…fit."

Alice goes back to helping Davy with the puzzle before I can figure out how to respond.

Cam and I make our escape shortly after that, his mom waving and shouting, "Have a good time!" and "Take lots of pictures!" as we head down the front walk. She doesn't vanish back into the house until we're in the car with the doors closed.

When the front door shuts behind her, I burst out laughing, and Cam joins me.

"Wow." I lean my head back against the cushioned headrest of Cam's mom's SUV. "That was pretty intense."

"I am so sorry," Cam says. "I tried to warn you."

"No warning could've prepared me for that. Anyway, it wasn't all bad. It was kind of fun, actually." I wrestle with myself, decide not to say anything, and then say it anyway. "It kind of made me wish I was your date for real."

Cam was turning the key in the ignition, but at that he goes completely still.

"I know we're not talking about this yet," I rush to say, "but that's how I felt. It's how I feel."

Cam's voice is soft. "You can't say things like that, Jasper."

"Why not?"

He swallows. "You know why not."

He starts the car, and the SUV takes us down the road more smoothly than my old clunker ever could. We pull up to Felix's house, and I can't deny he looks amazing in a tailored black suit with a silver tie. I slide into the backseat with him—he is my date, after all, and my boyfriend—and he leans in to kiss me on the same cheek Cam kissed earlier. Cam's eyes lock onto us in the rearview mirror before he looks away.

Since Raven and Lars are next-door neighbors, Cam pulls the SUV to a stop between their houses and texts both of them that we've arrived. Raven emerges first, looking gorgeous in a floor-length purple gown with a sequined bodice, and I'm wondering if Lars has changed their mind about joining us when their front door opens, and they step outside.

Felix sucks in a breath.

Lars's hair is full and wavy, hanging in silky white-blond waves to their chin. Light contouring makeup highlights both their square jaw and more delicate features, and the addition of artful eyeliner makes their eyes look impossibly blue. A cream-colored gown flows down over their slim body like a gossamer waterfall, clinging to their torso and then flaring out in a full skirt that swishes when they walk. Black combat boots peek out beneath the skirt, and the dark blue blazer patterned with stars and bluish-purple galaxies is so perfectly Lars I'm not surprised Felix stares as he pushes open the car door.

Lars gathers their skirt and climbs in, and Felix obligingly moves to the middle seat to make room for them. Up close, Lars looks even more stunning, and the entire car is silent as we stare at them.

Lars laughs self-consciously as they buckle their seat belt. "What? Say something, you guys are freaking me out."

Raven shakes her head from the front passenger seat. "You couldn't let me be the prettiest one, could you? You just had to show up looking like a freakin' supermodel."

Lars blinks at her. "Um, what?"

"Don't 'um, what' me. You look *gorgeous*, you jerk."

Lars's cheeks flush. "No, I don't."

"You really do." There's a stunned fervor to Felix's voice that makes me wonder if he's finally realizing that Lars is, in fact, really freaking attractive. "Seriously."

The soft, secret smile that comes to Lars's lips isn't lost on me, and neither is the fact that as we pull back onto the road, Felix keeps looking over at them like he can't keep his eyes away.

The ride to the school is filled with light chatter and laughter. Every now and then I catch Cam looking at me through the mirror, and I wonder what he's thinking, if his brain is caught up in the memory of his lips on my cheek like mine is. Mostly, though, I keep my attention on Felix and Lars. Their conversation goes a mile a minute, and even though Felix occasionally turns my way to keep me included, it feels like the world has narrowed around him and Lars and shut everything else out.

When we pull into the school parking lot and settle into a space, Felix automatically reaches for Lars's hand to help them out of the SUV. Lars's face softens as their hands touch, and once they're both out of the car, there's a moment when their eyes track down to their joined hands, and they both give a little start and pull their fingers away from each other. But I can tell by their faces it felt right.

Them together, it's just *right*.

The gym is decorated with colorful streamers and a huge sign proclaiming, "Nelson Springs High Homecoming Dance," in case anyone wandered in by mistake and had no idea what they'd stumbled onto. There's a DJ set up at the far end of the room, a wide space for dancing, and a series of tables with punch and snacks and little pastries I'm sure are nowhere near as good as Cam's mom's. Chairs line the walls, but most people are out on the dance floor jumping around to some high-energy pop song I've heard on the radio but couldn't name if my life depended on it.

My first instinct is to beeline for the snacks table and then find a place to sit. But Lars, Felix, and Raven are already heading for the dance floor, so I exchange resigned smiles with Cam and follow them.

We last for a decent amount of songs, but finally Cam and I have to call it quits. We make our excuses to the others and head wearily over to the punch bowl, where a bored-looking teacher pours out two plastic cups of fruity liquid.

Cam and I find seats at the far corner of the gym where the music decibel level is low enough that we can hear each other without shouting.

"I'm just not built for dancing," I say when I can form words again. "My body doesn't move that way, and I don't think it wants to."

Cam downs his punch and studies me with an amused lift of his eyebrow. "I don't know, you didn't look too bad out there."

"You have many talents, Mr. Matsumoto-Rogers, but lying is not one of them. Still, I appreciate the thought."

Cam opens his mouth to answer, but his pocket buzzes and he wrestles out his phone. His fingers fly over the screen, and then he tucks the phone back into his pocket and leans back in his chair with a pleased smile.

"What?" I ask.

He blinks at me and scratches sheepishly at the back of his head. "So I may have done some meddling…"

As if on cue, the gym doors open, and Jess strides in. She's wearing an amazing cherry-red suit and tie that somehow don't clash with her hair, and she throws Cam a double thumbs-up as she crosses to the dance floor.

"Oh my God," I say. "Cam, what did you do? How did you even know?"

He shrugs. "Raven's my friend, and I pay attention. And it's not like I *did* anything exactly. I just mentioned to Jess that Raven was going to be at the dance, and that if there was anything she might want to say to her, this would be a good chance to say it."

I watch, oddly apprehensive for everyone involved, as Jess marches over to Raven—who is still dancing with Felix and Lars—and taps her on the shoulder. Raven turns around, and her eyes widen almost comically as her gaze falls on Jess. She folds her arms protectively over her chest as Jess talks to her, then ducks her head and says something in response.

"I wish we had subtitles or something," Cam says, and I wholeheartedly agree.

Raven and Jess exchange a few more words, and then Jess takes Raven's arm and leads her off the dance floor, across the gym, and toward the door to the back hallway. As they pass us, Raven mouths, *Oh my God*, and Jess throws Cam a wink, and then the door closes behind them and they're gone.

A few minutes pass during which I try not to wonder about what might be happening out in the hallway, but I end up seeing all I need to the next time the door opens. Raven and Jess are tucked in the nook by the soda machine, arms around each other and lips pressed warmly together.

When the two of them slip back into the gym hand in hand, Jess's voice reaches my ears over the music. "—kept running away, so I thought you didn't like me." Raven replies, "I kept running away *because* I liked you!" and they both burst out laughing as they head for the dance floor. I knock my cup of punch against Cam's, and we drink a toast to Raven and Jess.

Felix and Lars track us down maybe half an hour later, at which point Cam and I are laughing about his mom, who is apparently an even worse dancer than him or me, stumbling during a conga line and doing a full-on belly flop into a three-tier wedding cake.

"Hey," Felix says. His cheeks are flushed, his entire body seeming to vibrate with energy and elation. Lars is equally rosy-cheeked and bright-eyed as they sip from a bottle of water. "Feel like giving the dance floor another try?"

I groan and lean my head back against the wall, and Cam laughs.

"I mean during a slow song," Felix says with a smiling roll of his eyes. "There ought to be one coming up soon. What do you say?"

I force myself not to glance at Cam as I nod. "Yeah, sure."

Despite Felix's prediction, no slow song is forthcoming for a while, so he and Lars hang out with Cam and me while we sip our drinks and try to find things to converse about as a group. It starts out decently well as we share cheerful gossip about Raven and Jess, but before long, we've split into two separate conversations, Cam and I talking excitedly about the new Indian restaurant that just opened up downtown while Felix and Lars fall into an animated "who would win in a fight" argument about their respective sci-fi franchises.

"They have the *Force*," Felix says. "They could just wave their hands and take them all out."

"Then why didn't they wave their hands and take down the Empire? If they couldn't defeat a bunch of foot soldiers who can't shoot worth crap, no way they could take out a race of super strong cyborgs with crazy-advanced technology. They'd get assimilated in a second, and then there'd be super strong cyborgs *with the Force*. Nobody would stand a chance against them."

Felix folds his arms and glares at Lars, but the corners of his mouth twitch upward. "I refuse to accept that."

"Because you don't like that it's the truth?"

Felix presses his lips together. "Maybe."

He and Lars laugh, and I realize Cam is watching me watch them. I smile to show him I'm okay, and I think he gets it. When a slow song comes on the speakers a moment later, Felix blinks and shakes himself like he's woken from a dream. The two of us get up to dance, and to my surprise, Cam holds an arm out to Lars.

"Want to dance?"

Lars blinks in surprise and glances at Felix, but then they smile. "Sure. But I'm leading."

Felix loops his arm in mine, and as we take our place on the dance floor, we pass Jess and Raven with their arms around each other and equally radiant smiles on their faces. I've never seen Raven with such a light, easy expression, as if all the stress and responsibility she usually carries around has vanished. As she and Jess dance, Jess gently brushes a hair away from Raven's face, and I wonder if Raven might be about to melt from happiness.

Felix and I find an empty spot among the couples and get into position, his hands on my waist and mine on his shoulders. It's my first time dancing with a boy in public, and I feel like I should probably be paying more attention to it. But as Felix and I sway to the music, my gaze keeps drifting over his shoulder to Cam. He and Lars march back and forth across the floor like this is a tango, dipping each other every few steps and mightily annoying the couples trying to enjoy a romantic moment in their vicinity.

I can't help laughing, and Felix gives me a confused smile.

"What?"

"Cam and Lars."

Felix glances over his shoulder and laughs, too. Again, there's that brightness to his eyes I only ever see when he looks at Lars.

It's nice being close to him. My senses fill with the warm cedar scent of his cologne, and it feels good to have his hands on my waist, his face so close to mine. But my heart isn't racing, and I'm not dreaming of holding him close and kissing him.

I let out a long breath. "Felix…"

"Jas," he says at the same moment, and we laugh awkwardly.

"You go ahead," I say.

He looks uncertain but nods. "I was just going to

say… Is there something a little off with us?"

I swallow and don't meet his eyes. "What do you mean?"

"I mean, like today. This dance. I'm having fun, and I think you are, too. But is it kind of weird we're not having fun together?"

Oh, God, this is it. We're doing this.

"It's not weird." I take a deep breath. "If we're friends. Friends hang out with each other sometimes, and sometimes they don't, and it's fine either way. But if we're boyfriends…then yeah, it's a little weird you're having a better time with Lars, and I'm having a better time with…with Cam."

Felix's eyes widen. "Oh," he says softly.

We sway in silence for a bit.

"I do love you," Felix says. "I always have."

"I love you, too."

"But not…like that?"

I squeeze my eyes shut and wish we were past this, that there was a way to skip this moment and the inevitable hurt it's going to cause. "No. Not like that."

I brace myself for the return of cold, angry Felix, but he just sighs and says, "Yeah, same here, I think."

My eyes snap open. "You… Really?"

"I really wanted this to be *it,* you know? It just made sense. I loved you back then, I love you now, and you were my first kiss, the first boy I ever wanted to kiss. But I don't think I want to be with you like that. It feels good when I'm with you, but when we're not together, I'm not thinking about you all the time or wishing I could be with you again. I'm not dreaming about kissing you. It's not that I don't miss you, but I don't *miss* you—does that make any sense? I mean, it doesn't even bother me seeing you with Cam, and I think it probably should because it's pretty clear you guys like each other a lot."

"And you like Lars," I say.

Felix goes still. "What?"

I can't help laughing at the dumbstruck look on his face. "Come on, you two are practically made for each other. I've never seen you happier than when you're with them, and you looked like you were about to faint when they showed up tonight in that gown."

Felix's face goes a bit pink. "They look great, yeah, but I mean, I didn't... I never..."

"Felix," I say in a flat voice.

He sighs. His gaze drifts over my shoulder, and his expression softens. "They are pretty amazing."

"Yeah, and it's clear they think the same about you."

The pleased smile growing on Felix's face tells me all I need to know.

"Huh." He looks at me with a sudden twinge of apprehension. "We can still be friends after this, right? I mean, just because we don't like each other *like that* doesn't mean we have to stop hanging out together, right?"

"What? Yeah, of course we'll still be friends! Do you really think I spent all this time trying to make up with you to just ditch you? Sorry to break it to you, but you're stuck with me now, probably forever. Six years was enough without my best friend."

A faint sheen of tears shines in Felix's eyes before he blinks them away. "Good. And you know, I don't regret any of this. Kissing you, being your boyfriend for a little while... It's the only reason I was able to do any of what I did this week. Come out, join the QSA, stand up to Tyler, all of it. I feel like I'm myself again, and it's all because of you. Maybe I was only your boyfriend for a little while, but it changed my whole life."

"*You* changed your whole life. And if dating me was the push you needed to do that, then it was all worth it."

He beams at me, and I realize the song we're swaying to is coming to an end. When the music fades out, Felix pulls me in for a hug, and I cling to him for a long, warm moment, my face buried in the shoulder of the first boy who ever kissed me. And then I let him go.

Another slow song starts as we make our way over to where Lars and Cam are laughing together, having just finished their tango.

"Um, hey," I say.

Cam's gaze flickers between Felix and me, and a soft light of comprehension enters his eyes. Before he can say anything, Felix straightens his shoulders and holds his hand out to Lars.

"Would you want to dance with me?" There's a breathless note to his voice, a flush in his cheeks I hope Lars picks up on.

Lars's eyes go wide, and they look sharply at me. I take a small but decided step away from Felix, and Lars stares at Felix like they're seeing him for the first time.

"I… Yeah." They laugh lightly and step forward. "Sure, Felix."

Lars tentatively takes Felix's hand, and they make their way across the dance floor without ever taking their eyes off of each other.

"So…" Cam stuffs his hands into his pockets and lifts his eyebrows. "Are we dancing, too, or is that just reserved for the people who actually know how?"

I open my mouth to say yes, then close it again. "Actually, do you want to go outside with me for a little bit?"

Chapter Twenty-Five

I want to take Cam's hand, but a rush of shyness and nerves stops me. Instead, I lead the way through the crowd of couples, past the snack table, and out the exterior side door of the gym. The cool night air feels amazing after the muggy closeness inside, and I draw in a long, brisk lungful as Cam and I sit down on the cold concrete of the steps.

We drift in a comfortable silence for a bit, my shoulders feeling lighter than they have in a long time. Felix is going to be okay. *Felix and I* are going to be okay. And hopefully Cam and I will be something even better.

"So Felix and I had a talk," I say.

Cam's tone is carefully neutral. "Oh yeah?"

"Yeah."

"So what did you two talk about?"

"Oh, you know, the usual. The dance, the punch, how we both like someone else."

Cam's eyebrows shoot upward. "Really."

"Really."

"So Felix likes Lars?"

"Yep."

"And this person you like…"

"Yeah?"

He grins and folds his arms. "What are they like?"

"You're really going to make me say it?"

"Yep."

"Fine. They're pretty amazing, actually. Seriously the best friend I've ever had, and such a ridiculously nice person it took me a really long time to figure out they might have feelings for me."

Cam laughs. "Oh, so it's their fault?"

"I didn't say that. I'm just saying, when somebody's friendly with literally everyone, it's hard to figure out if they like you *like that*."

"Fine, I'll accept that. Go on."

"So this person I like…they're always there for me, and they've been like that pretty much since the second we met. They're always the first person to notice if something's bothering me, and they actually care about what I have to say, even when it's kind of dumb."

"I can't remember you ever saying anything I thought was dumb."

"That time I rambled for twenty minutes about how there needs to be a super-fast train line under the ocean so people who can't afford airfare can still travel?"

A fond smile plays on Cam's lips. "That wasn't dumb, it was passionate. And you made a lot of good points. Though I hope you know that any trips you took on the underwater train would be done without me. I would not be caught dead on a train that went under the ocean, even if Elvis himself was the conductor."

"Noted. The point is, you're way too nice to me, and you have been since I met you. And if I'm honest with myself, I guess I've been thinking about you in a more-than-friends way for a while now. I always shut it down because I figured you'd never feel the same way, and I was so focused on Felix. But I always felt it, and I'm sorry it took me so long to realize it."

Cam's eyes are bright as he shakes his head. "You don't have to apologize."

I turn my body to face him, my hands dropping to my sides. "Maybe not, but I want to. And I also... There's something else I want to do. If it's okay with you."

He goes still, and I know he understands what I'm asking. He nods, and a rush of nervous anticipation trembles through me.

I trace my fingers along his face, following the same path his fingertips trailed down my cheek last night. He closes his eyes and leans into my touch, and when his eyes open again, they're dark and full and just a little needy.

There's an eternal moment before our lips touch when my mind is racing and my heart is pounding and I wonder if this is actually going to live up to everything I've dreamed it would be. But then Cam's mouth presses against mine, and it turns out it's not everything I've dreamed of. It's more.

Cam's lips are soft and move achingly slowly against mine, teasing over my top lip and then caressing my bottom lip with a gentle, building pressure. The same electric tingle I felt when our hands brushed in class jolts through me, and I press closer and wrap my arms around him. His arms go snugly around me in return, and it's all the warmth and solidity of a Cam hug but with the added bonus of his mouth moving against mine, his breath against my lips, his everything all intertwined with mine.

We pull back and look at each other, and he smiles, and I smile, and then he leans in and kisses more deeply, more hungrily. He said before he's been interested in me since we met, but this is the first time I really feel it.

There's a sense of pent-up restraint finally being released, and he kisses me like he's been wanting to for years instead of weeks.

I kiss him back just as desperately, and it's a long time before we come up for air.

He leans his forehead against mine, eyes closed and breath coming fast, and because I can, I brush a strand of hair back from his face.

"You have no idea," he breathes, "how many times I've wanted to do that."

I smile. "And?"

He opens his eyes and meets my gaze. "Totally worth the wait."

I want to kiss him again, or maybe just wrap my arms around him and never let go, but the steady thrum of music from the gym cuts out, and shouts echo from inside. Cam and I burst back through the gym door just as Tyler Bruce crashes to the floor at our feet.

It turns out to be Lars, not Felix, who stands above Tyler shaking out their fist. Felix sits on the floor a few feet away, blood seeping out of his nose while Raven examines him and Jess pulls a wad of tissues from her pants pocket.

Tyler's cheek is already purpling as he climbs to his feet and spins around to face Lars. "What the hell, Henry?"

"What, you think just because I'm wearing a dress I can't punch you?" Lars has drawn themselves up to their full height, and they look beautiful and a little terrifying as they glare at Tyler.

Tyler takes a threatening step forward, but Cam catches his shoulder. One glance back at Cam looming over him, and Tyler goes still.

"Look, whatever!" Tyler directs his words to where Felix is bleeding into Jess's tissues. "Be gay, dance with some freak in a dress, I don't care. Just don't act like you can't stand me all of a sudden, okay? You're my best friend, Morales! We've been best friends for years, and now it's like you don't even care!"

The tissues stuffed into Felix's bleeding nose makes his voice weird and muffled. "Jesus, is that what this is about? You're jealous?"

Tyler's face goes red. "I'm not in love with you or anything, man. I just don't get why you can't be friends with these losers and also with me."

Felix sighs. "It'd probably help if you stopped calling them losers and freaks, for a start."

A squad of teachers finally shows up, I assume after the sole teacher on punch bowl duty ran for backup, and one of them takes Tyler by the arm while the other tends to Felix and Lars. I have a moment of fear for Lars, who could very well get suspended right along Tyler for fighting, but they just look grimly pleased as the teachers lead the group out of the gym. Raven and Jess trail after them, trying to explain what happened to the teachers.

Cam and I exchange glances, then grab each other's hands and hurry after our friends. The music starts back up and people wander back to the dance floor, though there's a lot of murmuring and several people glancing toward the hallway door and shaking their heads. The snatches of conversation I catch all seem to be firmly anti-Tyler. Even the soccer team guys look disgusted at his behavior, which is not something I ever expected.

Cam and I find Felix, Lars, and Tyler sitting on the long bench in the hallway, Lars with an ice pack on their hand, Felix with one pressed to his nose, and Tyler scowling and holding one to his cheek. Raven and Jess are a few feet away still pleading their case to the teachers. Raven looks like she's in full Vice President Raven mode, and Jess keeps throwing her impressed, besotted looks.

"I'm not saying we can't be friends," Felix says as Cam and I approach. "I'm just saying you can't act like a homophobic prick to other people and expect me to be okay with that. I don't want to be friends with somebody who acts like that, so if you want to be my friend, you're gonna have to act like a decent human being, man."

Before Tyler can reply, Ms. Darby, the stern older lady who teaches Social Studies and who I personally would never want to mess with, marches over in her navy blue pantsuit and matching canvas sneakers. Raven and Jess trail after her, holding hands and looking pleased.

Ms. Darby levels a solemn look at the three perpetrators. "We'll be calling each of your parents and asking them to come to pick you up. Of course we'll have to see what the principal says about this, but from what I've heard from Ms. Jacobs and—" She glances sideways at Raven and Jess. "—these rather outspoken young ladies, it seems Tyler started the fight unprovoked, and Lars was defending himself."

"Themself," Felix says.

Ms. Darby blinks. "Excuse me?"

"Lars is nonbinary," Felix says. "They/them pronouns."

Ms. Darby stares at him like she's not sure he's speaking English, but finally she gives a grudging nod. "In any case, I can say pretty definitively that Mr. Bruce, you'll be facing an out-of-school suspension. Mr. Morales, you're in no trouble whatsoever since all you

215

did was get hit in the face, and Mr…"

"Just Lars," Lars says with a small smile.

"Lars," Ms. Darby says, arching an eyebrow, "will most likely be exonerated due to extenuating circumstances, but we'll know the final verdict on Monday. Now, I hope all three of you will refrain from getting into any further scuffles until your parents arrive, and if you do feel the need to resort to violence, please consider removing yourselves from school property so I won't have to deal with it."

She spins on her heel and walks away, and Lars reaches over with their free hand to intertwine their fingers with Felix's.

"Thanks," they say softly.

Felix's smile is warm and bright and shining with affection.

I lean into Cam and slide my arm around him, and there's no hesitation before he wraps his arm around me and holds me close.

"So." I can't hold back a smile, but that's okay, because everyone except Tyler is grinning like an idiot right now, anyway. "Best dance ever?"

Chapter Twenty-Six

Raven ends up hitching a ride with Jess. They've barely taken their eyes or their lips off each other all night, so I'm not exactly sure how Jess is intending to drive, but I'm sure she'll figure it out. And Felix and Lars both have to be driven home by their parents, so it's just Cam and me in the SUV after the dance.

I still can't quite believe how much everything has changed over the last few hours, but I get all the confirmation I need when Cam doesn't let go of my hand as we drive. He also keeps glancing over at me with a warm, loving smile on his face I'm sure I'm returning tenfold.

When we pull into my driveway, I'm not ready to say goodnight yet. I mean, frankly I'd be happy if I never had to be away from him ever again, and it hits me all over again that I never felt this way with Felix, and that probably should've been a clue.

"Hey, so you can absolutely say no to this," I say, "but any chance you'd want to sleep over at my house tonight?"

Cam's eyes go wide, and I rush to explain.

"I don't mean… I just want to keep hanging out with you, and we can even sleep in different rooms if you're not comfortable—"

"Jasper, it's fine." He sounds amused. "I get it. And yeah, I'll check with my mom, but I'm pretty sure it'll be okay. Do you want to maybe ask your dad first, though?"

"Right. Right. I should probably do that." I reach for the car door handle, then turn back and kiss him because no way am I getting out of this car without doing that. "Be right back."

He gives a light, pleased laugh, and I hurry up the walk to the house. I'm calling, "Dad!" as I open the front door, but it's not my dad I see when I walk into the kitchen.

She's sitting at the table when I enter, wearing a satiny red blouse and black jeans. Her thick brown hair hangs in a loose braid over one shoulder, and she looks tanner, happier. Her eyes fill with smiling tears as she gets to her feet.

"*Mi amor,*" she says.

I stare at her. "Mom."

She takes an aborted step toward me, arms lifting as if to hug me, then seems to think better of it and just looks at me instead. I realize I walked past a rolling suitcase by the front door when I came in, and I wonder how long she's staying, if Dad knew she was coming, what her presence here even means.

Before I can figure out how to react, there's the sound of feet on the stairs, and Dad jogs into view. His expression is taut, and I can tell by the helpless way he looks at me that he's as surprised as I am to have Mom sitting in our kitchen. His gaze flickers over to her before fixing on my face, and I wonder if it's hard for him to see her after all this time. It sure as hell is for me.

"How was the dance?" he asks.

Said dance already feels like a lifetime ago, but I manage a jerky nod. "Yeah, good. It was good."

"You look very handsome," Mom chimes in. Her

accent sounds a little thicker, something that always happens after she's spent time back in Spain. "Who is the lucky girl?"

Dad and I exchange glances, and I decide to ignore her completely for the time being.

"Uh, so Cam is out in the car. I was actually coming to ask if he could stay over tonight?"

Dad's gaze flickers over to Mom, but he smiles and rests his hand on my shoulder. "He's always welcome here, you know that. Tell him to come on in."

I nod and dash for the door, pretending not to hear Mom's protests that she would rather talk to me without a stranger present. Cam is leaning against the side of the car, scrolling on his phone when I get out there. He takes one look at my face and gives a worried frown.

"Are you okay? What happened?"

I shake my head wordlessly and fall into him. His arms go around me, and he holds me close without asking questions, for which I am extremely grateful.

"My mom is here," I mumble into his shoulder. "She just asked me what girl I took to the dance, and I really don't know if I can deal with having her here, but she's here so I guess I'll have to deal with it. And Dad said you can still stay over, but I completely understand if you don't want to because there's going to be some family drama going on here for sure, and I would seriously not blame you if you wanted to just—"

"Jasper," Cam cuts in before I can spiral any further. "Hey. Of course I still want to stay. If you're sure you want me to."

"I definitely do. Honestly, if you'd said no, I probably would've asked if I could go home with you instead, because I do not want to face this alone right now."

He holds me tighter. "You won't."

I don't make any move to separate from him, and after a while he rocks us back and forth with little bouncing movements that almost coax a smile from me.

"You know we're going to have to go in there eventually," he murmurs into my hair.

I press my face to his chest. "I know."

"Your parents are probably wondering what's taking so long."

That finally gets through to me, and I step back. The last thing I need is for Mom to walk out here and see me locked in a loving embrace with a boy, or for Dad to forbid Cam from sleeping over because we're not safely in the "just friends" category anymore.

Cam squeezes my shoulder, and even though it's not as good as a hug, it helps. "It's gonna be okay," he says. "And even if it's not, we'll get through it."

The "we" means a lot to me, and I wonder, not for the first time, how I ever got so lucky as to end up with Cam in my life.

I steel myself as best I can and head back into the house.

****

The last time I saw Mom was the day she left us.

Things had been coming to a head for a while, and the last straw was the Father James ambush at the Christmas service. Mom came home that day cold and furious after getting one of her friends to drive her home, and I heard her and Dad arguing late into the night. At least, I heard her arguing—Dad's voice, even in arguments, was always quiet, so I could never make out his words, but I definitely heard hers.

"It's like you don't even care! Our son is turning into some kind of deviant, and that doesn't bother you?"

Low murmurs from my dad.

"Then what would you call it? I think we should take away his internet. It's clearly having a bad influence on him. And I think he should start coming to church with me again, and spending more time with people who can be a good influence. Father James mentioned a camp for boys like him, and I really think—"

Dad said something sharp.

"Well, he's my son, too, Julian! I can't just stand by and let this happen!"

I listened for a while longer, then jammed my earbuds into my ears and pressed my pillow over my head. The muffled echo of my mother's voice was still ringing in my ears when I fell asleep.

The next week was difficult. I was off school until after New Year's, so I had nowhere to go, and Mom stalked around the house fuming silently and not speaking to Dad or me. I woke up on New Year's Eve to find her red suitcases stacked by the front door.

I tuned out most of what she said, but I caught a few words like "priorities," "compromise," and "sinful paths." She stood straight-backed and upright in her nicest church clothes—a crimson skirt suit with a ruffled white blouse, pantyhose, and matching red heels—while the gold cross necklace nestled against her throat glittered in the morning sunlight.

Dad kept his arm around me as she spoke, his jaw tight and his fingers pressing hard into my shoulder. When Mom paused at the end of her tirade, clearly waiting for us to beg her to stay, Dad walked calmly to the front door and flung it open.

She didn't tell me she loved me. She didn't hug me or kiss me or reassure me that no matter how she felt right now, she was still my mom. She just looked at me with sixteen years' worth of disappointment, picked up her suitcases, and left.

Dad hugged me hard after she was gone, and I hugged him back feeling numb. Was I sad? I figured I must be, but I didn't feel like crying, and when I thought about waking up the next day to a house free of my mother's presence, all I could think was, *Thank God.*

****

Luckily, Cam has his gym clothes in the trunk of the SUV, so he's able to change out of his suit and into a gray T-shirt and sweatpants that smell only faintly of duffel bag. I trade my own suit for a pair of striped pajama pants and a T-shirt with the Eiffel Tower on it, then place my hand on my bedroom doorknob and don't turn it.

When ten or fifteen seconds pass like this, Cam takes my hand and draws it gently back from the knob. "If you don't want to talk to her right now, we could say we're wiped out from the dance and want to go right to sleep."

I shake my head wearily. "I'm still not going to want to talk to her in the morning, so we might as well get it over with now. Anyway, if I have to face her, I think I'd feel better doing it when you're around. Is that too clingy?"

He shoots me a fond but exasperated look. "We've been going out for maybe two hours, and you're already worrying about being clingy?"

"I can't help it. I worry about these things."

"Well, don't."

He kisses me, and it's sweet and soft and makes every nerve ending in my body tingle.

"God, why did we waste a whole month *not* kissing?"

Cam laughs. "It wasn't my idea, believe me."

He squeezes my hand, and together we head downstairs.

Mom and Dad are talking quietly at the kitchen table when we enter the room, our hands carefully not touching. Dad's posture is tense, a deep line between his eyebrows. When he catches sight of Cam and me, he jumps to his feet and turns his back on Mom.

"So you boys feel like a snack, or do you want to head straight to bed?"

For a second I really am tempted to put this off until morning. But I'd just spend all night worrying, and it'd be nice to actually sleep tonight.

"Uh, sure, a snack sounds good," I say. "Popcorn?"

Dad's already pulling the air popper out of the cabinet. "Jasper, why don't you sit and have a chat with your mom, and Cam can help me get this set up. You don't mind, do you, Cam?"

Cam stirs beside me. "No, of course not. Happy to help."

His hand brushes along my back as he goes to help my dad, and the message is clear. *I'm here if you need me.*

Feeling like I'm walking to the guillotine instead of the kitchen table, I pull out my usual chair and sit down.

Mom beams at me again, and I tense up, wondering why she's so happy to see me. It's pretty messed up that my first instinct is to feel suspicious when my mother actually looks pleased to be in the same room as me, but here we are.

"So how's Pablo?" I ask. I don't care one way or another, but I figure I should at least be civil.

"He's wonderful." Her voice is warm and bubbly, a tone I haven't heard directed at me in a very long time. "He just got a raise at work, and it's going to be so helpful in paying for the wedding."

This jars me even though it shouldn't. "The wedding?"

Happy tears fill her eyes again, and she reaches across the table to grab my hand. "Yes, darling, Pablo and I are getting married. Next spring. And we want you to be there."

I eye her warily. "In Spain?"

"Yes, of course. Where else would we get married? It's going to be a beautiful ceremony, and all the family will be there, but it just wouldn't be the same without my little boy there as well. And—" Her eyes sparkle. "—Pablo has a niece who would be just perfect for you, so pretty and smart. We were thinking you two could be paired together in the ceremony and then, who knows? Perhaps something will bloom!"

Dad drops the popcorn bowl, and the kitchen fills with the ringing clatter of it rolling all over the countertop. I feel Cam's eyes on me, but I don't turn to look at him. I watch my mom, taking in the willfully ignorant happiness on her face, the genuine belief that I would be freaking delighted to hear she wants to set me up with a girl.

Over the last few years, I could never find the courage to say the words to her. Even on the day she left us, even knowing she already knew about me, I couldn't say them. But it turns out all the months away from her have given me the distance I need.

I pull my hand back from hers and sit taller in my chair. "Mom, I don't want to be set up with some girl from Spain. I'm gay."

The smile vanishes from her face, but it's back a second later, only slightly strained.

"You say that now, but you haven't met Francesca."

"I don't need to meet Francesca. Look, please, trust me. I could meet a thousand Francescas, and I'd still have zero interest in them because I'm just not interested in girls."

"A lot of boys feel like that when they're young, but you'll change your mind when you're older, once you grow up a bit and realize—"

"No, I won't!" I'm on my feet now, hands clenched at my sides. "Mom, please. I need you to *listen*. If you really want me at your wedding, I'll go, but it has to be as me, not as this straight fantasy version of me you've built up in your head. If I go to your wedding, it'll be as your gay son, because that's who I am. And I'll probably want to bring my boyfriend with me, too, because I'm not ashamed of who I am or who I love. If you can't deal with that, then maybe you should turn right around and fly back to Spain. Because if you're not going to accept me for who I am, then maybe I don't want you in my life."

I'm panting by the time I'm done, dreading my mom's response but so glad I finally said the words I've been holding in for all these years. *This is who I am. You can't change me, so either accept me or leave me alone.*

While Mom is still staring at me, eyes wide and mouth hanging open, Dad comes up behind me and puts his arm around my shoulders. He doesn't say anything, but he doesn't need to. He's there, and it means the world to me.

Mom wobbles to her feet, her eyes bright with unshed tears. "I hoped you would've grown out of this by now, Jasper." Her voice is soft and wounded, the *you've hurt me* version of itself that always cut right to the heart of me when I was a kid. It does the same to me now even though I know she's using it to manipulate me. "I've been praying about this every single day, and so has Pablo. We both love you so much, and we only want what's best for you. That's another reason why I'm here. Not just to ask you to our wedding, but to ask you to come live with us."

The words knock the breath out of me. "What?"

The warm and loving version of my mother is back, gazing at me with bright, earnest eyes. "Just think about it, sweetheart. You've always wanted to live in Europe, and now you can! Pablo and I have a beautiful little house, and you can go to school there, learn the language, have so many amazing experiences you could never have here."

Dad's arm goes rigid against my shoulders, but he doesn't say anything, and I know without asking that he already knew about this. She told him and it's killing him, but he's going to let me make my own decision because he's incredible like that.

Mom takes a step closer to me, her hands clasped in front of her, her gaze locked on mine like she's trying to will me into accepting. "It's not right, a child being away from his mother. And this place is no good for you, sweetheart. I know if you just come stay with me for a while, you'll be able to come back from this. You've been led astray, but there's no reason why you can't come back. You can still be *saved*, Jasper."

I wasn't considering the offer before this, not really. Living in Europe would be a dream, but leaving Dad? Leaving Cam? Felix, Raven, Lars, everyone I've gotten close to here? It's unthinkable. But with those words, the tiny flicker of hope that had kindled inside me fades and dies.

"So what you're saying is you want me to come live with you so you can change me," I say. "So you and Pablo can 'pray away the gay' or something."

"This is not who you are." The tears are back in Mom's eyes, the carefully calculated anguish making her voice ragged. "Do you think it's easy for me to wake up every day knowing my baby is living a life of sin? To know that someday I'm going to step into the gates of Heaven knowing my son will never join me there? That while I'm living in paradise, my little boy will be burning in—"

"Get out," Dad says.

Mom blinks. "What?"

His arm tightens around my shoulders, steady and full of quiet strength. "Get out. There's a motel down the road. I'll pay for your room, but you're not staying here."

"Julian, I'm just telling him the truth—"

"No." Dad's voice is steel. "It's not the truth. The only truth I hear is that you don't love our son enough to accept him for who he is, and until you can do that, you don't deserve to be in his life. I agreed to let you tell him why you came here, and you've done that, so I'm now asking you to please leave our home."

Mom stares at me with big, appealing dark eyes. "Jasper…"

"This is who I am," I whisper. "It's not wrong, and

I'm not ashamed of it. If you can't accept me, then I have nothing more to say to you."

There's a long moment when Mom stares at me, looking so heartbroken a part of me wants to apologize, beg for her forgiveness. But I don't, and neither does Dad, and after a while she spins on her heel and leaves the room. We hear her shrugging into her coat and picking up her suitcase, and then the front door opens, and she's gone.

Between one breath and the next, I'm on the floor crying into my dad's shirt. His arms go tight around me, and he murmurs vaguely soothing things, but the tears keep coming and nothing seems able to make them stop.

I knew she wouldn't accept me. I've always known. But it still freaking *hurts*.

It takes a long time, but finally my sobs subside to occasional sniffles and the tears clear enough for me to see I've made a pretty impressive wet spot on the front of Dad's T-shirt. He holds me quietly for a while, and then he rests his head on top of mine and heaves a deep sigh.

"Are you sure you don't want to move?" he asks. "I know it wouldn't be easy living with your mom again, but you're always talking about how much you want to live in Europe. I don't want to stand in your way if it's something you really want."

I blink blearily up at him. "This is the only place I want to be right now. And if I can't be in Europe as myself, I don't want to be there at all."

He ruffles my hair, and his smile is soft and proud. "Good. Because who you are is pretty spectacular, and anyone who asks you to change doesn't deserve your time. Even if she's your mom."

Dad helps me to my feet, and I realize I haven't seen or heard any sign of Cam for a while. I glance around, hoping he hasn't left, but Dad tilts his head toward the doorway.

"He went in the living room. I get the feeling he didn't want to intrude." His smile softens. "So you finally realized he's the one, huh?"

I stare at him. "Um. What do you mean?"

Dad rolls his eyes. "Please, I'm not blind. It's pretty obvious in the way you two look at each other. Which, to be fair, isn't that different from the way you looked at each other when you were 'just friends,' but there's definitely a difference. Also, I may have peeked outside and seen some definite *canoodling* going on, so…"

My cheeks burn. "*Dad,* God, canoodling?" And then worry streaks through me, and I look at him sharply. "He can still sleep over, though, right? I know it's different since we're together now, but I really just—"

"Easy," Dad says. "Yes, he can sleep over. And I'm even willing to be very understanding and let him stay in your room. But just remember that these walls are very thin, and your old dad will be listening to anything you two might get up to together, so maybe keep that in mind."

"Oh my *God.*"

He laughs and pats me on the shoulder. "Go on, go talk to your boyfriend. I'm going to head up to bed." He hesitates, then presses his palms to my cheeks and kisses me on the forehead like he used to when I was a kid. "I'm proud of you, Jasper. I know tonight wasn't easy for you, but you were fantastic. I couldn't be prouder you're my son."

I head to the living room with these words ringing

in my ears, and I find Cam sitting on Dad's recliner with his knees drawn to his chest. At the sight of me, he leaps to his feet.

"Hey." His voice is rough and croaky, like he's the one who spent the last half an hour crying instead of me. "Are you—"

"I'm okay," I say. "Well, no, that's obviously not true. But I *will* be okay. Look, do you want to go upstairs?"

He takes my hand, and the warm weight of his fingers in mine feels so good and so right.

When we get to my room, I push the door shut and lead the way over to my bed. I haven't brushed my teeth or washed my face or anything, but I still climb under the covers and motion for Cam to join me. He only hesitates a second before crawling in next to me.

I click off the bedside lamp, and we lay facing each other in the near-darkness. It's warm and cozy under the blankets, and the addition of Cam only enhances the sense of safety. I sigh out a breath and manage a weak smile.

"Pretty great sleepover so far, huh?"

He doesn't laugh. Instead, he shifts forward so he can wrap his arms around me and pull me close.

"You know you're not going to Hell, right?"

I choke out a laugh. "Yeah, of course."

His voice is soft and serious. "Really? Because when you hear something over and over again, especially from someone you love, sometimes it gets stuck in your head even if you know, rationally, that it's not true."

I open my mouth to deny it but can't.

"Like, for me," Cam goes on, "it was my weight. All through my childhood, my dad was always making comments about it, making it sound like no one would ever love me because I was heavy. And I knew he was wrong, but I still felt like... I still feel like he's right sometimes."

I pull back so I can look at him. "That's crazy. Cam, you're so amazing. I can't imagine anyone not loving you." My eyes widen as I realize what I've said, and I rush on, "People care about you for who you are, not what you look like. And for the record, not that it matters, but I think you look pretty freaking good without a shirt on."

He snorts out a laugh. "Okay, thanks? You look pretty good, too, as long as we're exchanging chest-related compliments. But that's not my point. My point is the messages we get from people, especially our parents, stick with us sometimes even when we don't want them to. Even when we know better. Like, I know no matter how much I weigh or what I look like, I'm worthy of love, but that doesn't stop me from feeling like that's not true sometimes. And even though you know, logically, that your mom is wrong with all of her 'being gay is a sin' and 'gay people go to Hell' stuff..."

I close my eyes. "I still kind of believe it sometimes."

I don't know if I even believe in God or Heaven or Hell or any of that, but there's still a little voice in the back of my head that sometimes whispers, *What if she's right?*

"So what do I do?" I ask.

Cam pulls me close again, and I nestle against his chest and enjoy the steady, comforting rhythm of his heartbeat against my ear.

"You think about this moment," he murmurs. "Any

time you start to doubt yourself, think about lying here with me, and how it felt. How it feels. And tell yourself that if God does exist, He'd never send someone to eternal torment just for being happy and in love."

Happy and in love. And I am, aren't I?

We are.

I know it won't be that simple, that undoing years of my mom's voice in my head could take a lifetime. But I also know Cam is right. How I feel right now, being with him—it's good and right and pure, and I can't imagine any world in which loving him could be wrong.

Chapter Twenty-Seven

A small part of me expects Mom to call or show up on our doorstep with tears and apologies, having finally seen the error of her homophobic ways. But of course, she doesn't. Dad tells me later she flew back to Barcelona the very next morning, and we don't hear from her again about the wedding. She sends me a birthday card in early December, and it's signed "Love, Mom," but there's no message inside, and the card itself is a generic one with a birthday cake and some candles that just say "Happy Birthday."

I stare at it until the candles blur, then slide it into my bottom desk drawer and try to forget about it.

Cam comes to pick me up around eleven, and I'm glad all over again that my birthday happened to fall on a Saturday this year. When I head downstairs, Dad is still washing dishes from my annual Big Birthday Brunch—featuring homemade waffles and breakfast burritos, since they're my favorites—but he drops the dishrag and wipes his hands when I thud from the stairs onto the kitchen tile.

"Cam here already?" he asks.

"Yep, he's outside."

"Well, before you go, I wanted to give you one last birthday present."

I frown because he already gave me a really nice pair of new sneakers and a fifty-dollar gift card for the mall.

But he's standing in front of me with a little grin on his face as he holds out a white envelope, so I shake off my confusion and open it.

Inside is a folded sheet of printer paper, which I stare at for a good ten seconds before the words on it make any sense.

"This… What is this?" I need to hear him say it, or I won't believe it's real.

"Well—" Dad leans in to point at the words I can clearly read on the paper. "—this is an itinerary of our upcoming trip to Europe. See, we'll arrive in London on the 18th, visit Paris, and maybe head down to one of the Christmas markets in Germany. And then we'll check out a few universities and finish our trip staying with Aunt Gertrude in Amsterdam."

"But…it's so much money."

"Well, maybe I've been saving up. And anyway, if we were going to your mom's wedding, we'd need to spring for a trip to Europe anyway, so why not spend it doing things we actually want to do?"

My finger slides down the list of plane reservations, from Julian Sinclair to Jasper Sinclair to the unmistakable Cameron Matsumoto-Rogers printed at the bottom of the page. Dad catches the direction of my gaze and grins.

"Yeah, I hope you don't mind, but I invited Cam to come along with us."

I launch myself at Dad and hug him, and he laughs and staggers back a step. "Mind? Dad, *thank you!* This is amazing! Thank you so much!"

He takes the envelope from my hand and winks at me. "No problem, kiddo. You deserve it. Now go have a fun birthday with your boyfriend. We can talk more about the trip later tonight."

I'm still grinning when I climb into the passenger seat of Cam's mom's SUV. Cam kindly turns the polka music down when I open the door, but I can still hear accordions as he leans in to kiss me. I fear I'm starting to unironically like the polka.

"Happy birthday," he says, even though he already sent me a text saying the same thing at six a.m. "Did your dad finally tell you, or are you just really happy to see me?"

"Both." I wrap my arms around him as best I can in the awkward confines of the car. "I seriously can't believe we're going to *Europe*. I've been wanting to go back there for so long, and Dad even said we can look at universities while we're there, and *you're* going to be there, and... It's just the best birthday present ever."

Cam throws me a teasing smile as he shifts the car into drive. "Well, I kind of don't want to give you my present now."

"It's the best birthday present from my *dad* ever," I amend. "The winning spot in the 'best birthday present from my boyfriend' category is still wide open."

It's a little snowy out, but thankfully nothing close to the torrent that assaulted us back during that freak snowstorm in September. It's weird to think that back then, Cam and I barely knew each other, and Felix was a closeted, cigarette-smoking homophobe, but I guess it just goes to show how quickly things can change.

Everyone is already waiting at the restaurant when we arrive. They've snagged the big booth at the back, and as Cam and I approach, hand in hand, Raven and Jess are sharing a chocolate milkshake with two straws, and Lars has their arm around Felix while the two of them ponder the menu with their heads leaning against one another. Honestly, all six of us are pretty nauseating, and I love it.

Lars spots us first. "The birthday boy approaches," they declare in their dry, amused voice, and Raven and Jess separate their lips from their straws for long enough to greet Cam and me.

Felix, meanwhile, gets to his feet and enfolds me in a hug, the kind that ends with multiple back slaps because no matter how uncloseted he might be now, he still spends a whole lot of time with sporty straight guys who slap each other's backs when they hug. I grin and slap his back enthusiastically in return.

Felix sighs as he steps away from me. "I did it again, didn't I?"

"It's fine," I laugh. "I kind of like it. Makes me feel like a real bro."

"That's fine for him," Lars says with a lift of an eyebrow, "but if you ever do that to me, we are breaking up on the spot."

Felix rolls his eyes, but he's smiling as he slides back into his seat. "Noted."

Lars and Felix shift over so there's room for Cam and me to sit down, and after we've had time to consult the menu, we flag down a server and put in our orders for pizzas and milkshakes. I'm not super hungry since my Big Birthday Brunch was, as advertised, pretty big, but it won't stop me from enjoying lunch from the best pizza place in town.

Once we all have some sort of beverage in front of us, Cam lifts his lemon-lime soda and waits until it's joined by Raven's lemon water, Jess's cola, Lars's pink lemonade, and Felix's glass of neon yellow. "I'd like to wish a very happy birthday to Jasper, who is finally old enough to see R-rated movies without being accompanied by a parent or guardian."

I laugh, Felix, Lars, Raven, and Jess cheer and clink their glasses together, and Cam turns to face me with such a look of open affection in his eyes I feel bizarrely like crying.

"I know I promised I wasn't going to give some awful, cheesy birthday toast…"

"But…" Raven prompts.

"*But*…I'd be remiss in my duties as your boyfriend if I didn't get at least a little cheesy in honor of your birthday. So here goes."

He takes a deep breath, and even though we're in a semi-crowded pizza place with our best friends around us, it feels like his words are meant just for me.

"Jasper. Sometimes I really can't believe this is my life. It's not like I was lonely before you moved here, not exactly, but there was always something missing. I know your birthday is a time when we're supposed to give you gifts, but you know what? You've already given me a pretty amazing gift just by existing. So thank you. Thank you for having a birthday, thank you for existing, and thank you for being the person I like being with more than anybody else in the world. You're amazing, and I love you so freaking much."

There's a long silence, me blinking back tears and Cam gazing into my eyes with that warm, adoring smile on his face. Then Raven buries her face in Jess's shoulder and chokes out, "Dammit, Cameron!" and we're all laughing again.

Jess wordlessly hands Raven a tissue, and there's a restaurant-inappropriate honking noise as Raven blows her nose.

Cam lifts his glass higher. "Happy birthday, Jasper!"

Everyone clinks their glasses together, and while our friends drink, Cam leans in and kisses me. I kiss him back, wrapping my arms tight around him and reminding myself that we're in a public place, and it would be bad form to sit here making out with my boyfriend for the next ten minutes.

Our pizzas arrive, and the afternoon speeds by as we laugh and talk and eat and slurp our milkshakes. Felix and Lars regale us with some of the highlights of soccer season, which ended two weeks ago with a championship game they won thanks to Lars's last-minute goal, and the rest of us nod and pretend to be interested while they both insist the other is the better player and the *real* star of the team.

Raven talks about ideas she has for upcoming QSA events, including some very cool plans for Trans Day of Visibility in March, and I babble for a good fifteen minutes about the upcoming Europe trip and what I'm hoping to see while we're there. The whole time I talk, Cam watches me with his chin resting on his hand and a contented smile on his face, which makes me feel warm all over. Then Jess tells us about the latest scandal in the marching band, which involves a startling after-hours tryst in the instrument room between Hailey Oswald and one of the drumline guys.

I wonder if anyone's told Tyler about it yet and consider asking Felix, but for all that he and Tyler are basically on friendly terms again—under the provision that Tyler continues not to be a homophobic jerk—they're not really close anymore. Felix spends most of his time with Lars and Cam and me and the rest of the

QSA, and he seems a lot happier for it. There are still the occasional unavoidable interactions with Mac and Muncher, who are surprisingly okay when they're not around Tyler, but for the most part, Felix is more QSA superstar than soccer god these days. It suits him a lot better, and it clearly hasn't made him any less effective of a soccer captain.

And really, things at school have never been better for the people in the QSA. I'm not saying bullying has disappeared as a pastime, but it's definitely down, and I've actually heard cheerleaders and football players and other "popular" kids call people out for being homophobic, which is not something I ever expected. QSA membership is way up, both for queer kids and supportive straight allies, and according to Cam's friend on the student council, the number of same-sex couples signing up for the winter formal is at an all-time high. It's not like school has become some queer paradise or something, but it's definitely a friendlier, safer place since Felix came out, and while I have no idea what will happen after he graduates in June, for now at least, everything is pretty great.

Once we've finished stuffing ourselves with pizza, everyone breaks out the birthday gifts, most of which are small things like a rainbow pencil case from Raven, a new travel book from Jess, a graphic tee of the London skyline from Lars, and a rattling box from Felix that ends up being the remains of a Lego set he borrowed from me when we were ten but never gave back.

I laugh and tell him it's perfect, because it is. I'm already looking forward to putting the pieces together again and seeing what they make.

And then it's Cam's turn, and he smiles and pulls

something out of his coat pocket.

It's a familiar yellow container. When I pry off the lid, I stare down at a perfect little bean bun face with brown "skin," big dark eyes, and a mass of curly black hair.

"Is that *me*?" I ask, flabbergasted.

Cam grins, but his gaze drops shyly from mine. "It's supposed to be, yeah."

Everyone else cranes their necks to look, but I'm too busy staring at my mini bean bun self to tilt it so they can see.

"Cam, did you make this?"

He nods. "Mom's been teaching me how to make some of the easier pastries, and I know how much you like the red bean ones, so I thought… Well, I thought you might like if I made one of you."

I realize he's actually nervous, afraid I won't like it, so I throw my arms around his neck. "It's amazing! Thank you! Seriously, I'm really impressed. I had no idea you were this good at baking."

"You might want to hold off on that until you've tasted it," he says, a pleased flush in his cheeks. "Anyway, I thought about just buying you something, but I figured you might like this better."

"I definitely do."

When I bite into my bean-filled likeness, I'm not at all surprised to discover it's delicious. It tastes almost exactly like the ones Cam's mom sells at the café every day, except better because I know Cam made it especially for me. The taste of it catapults me right back in time to that first day Cam and I met—getting paired up in English class, bonding over bean buns and bubble tea at his mom's café, walking home together in the glow of the setting sun. I remember how lucky I felt that Cam chose to be my friend that day, and now I feel about a thousand times luckier that he ended up also choosing to be my boyfriend.

When the waitstaff stop refilling our water glasses and start sending pointed glances at our occupation of the biggest booth in the place, everyone except me chips in to pay for the meal, shouting me down when I try to contribute my fair share. We wander outside feeling full and happy. Jess has her arm around Raven, Felix has his arm around Lars, and Cam and I have our arms around each other. We linger around the front of the pizza place for a while just talking before everyone finally filters off to their respective cars and drives off.

Instead of taking us down the familiar route back to my house, Cam flicks on his turn signal and brings us to a halt by the park. I frown but don't ask any questions, and he leads me down the snow-speckled paths and finally to the pond and playground at the far end of the walking trail. The clouds have cleared to make way for bright, wintry sunlight, and it glints on the playground equipment and twinkles on the light dusting of snow on the ground.

We stop at the edge of the playground, where kids bundled in winter coats laugh and shout as they ride the swings, climb the monkey bars, and just generally have a great time. Their parents sit together on a bench a few feet away, chatting while casting an occasional watchful eye toward their children.

I shoot Cam a quizzical look. "What exactly are we doing here?"

He faces me and rests his hands lightly on my shoulders. "Just something I've been wanting to do for a while."

He wraps his arms around me and kisses me, slowly and deeply like we're in an old Hollywood movie. Everything goes soft and quiet as I drift in the warm press of his lips.

When we pull apart, both of us are smiling.

"What was that about?" I ask breathlessly.

"Just thought you'd like a new memory of kissing a boy on a playground," Cam says.

The words jolt through me, and I glance around. Of course, no one is staring or pointing. A little girl glances at us standing with our arms around each other and then goes right back to playing, like nothing noteworthy is happening. One of the moms on the bench gives us a warm smile before turning back to her friends, but other than that, no one takes any notice of us at all.

Cam brushes the hair back from my forehead, and my chest fills with so much warmth and love it's hard to breathe for a second.

"You okay?" he asks.

I smile because I really am.

"Yeah," I say.

I lean in and press our lips together again, and it's even better the second time. We're just two boys who love each other sharing a kiss in the December sunshine, and everything is perfect.

A word about the author...

T.J. Baer is a queer, trans author of LGBTQ+ novels and short fiction. Born in Western Pennsylvania, he currently resides in his adopted hometown of Chicago with two cats and a well-stocked cupboard of tea. When not writing, T.J. can be found either discussing queer media on his YouTube channel or failing to escape from murderous ghosts on Twitch. You can learn more about his other titles (and see pictures of his cats) at tjbaer.com.